The Tunnel of
Hugsy Goode

The Tunnel of Hugsy Goode

By ELEANOR ESTES

Illustrated by Edward Ardizzone

Harcourt Brace Jovanovich, Inc.
New York

Library of Congress Catalog Card Number: 79-167833
ISBN 0-15-291100-6
Printed in the United States of America
First edition
B C D E F G H I J

To

C. and T.

Contents

The Tunnel of
Hugsy Goode

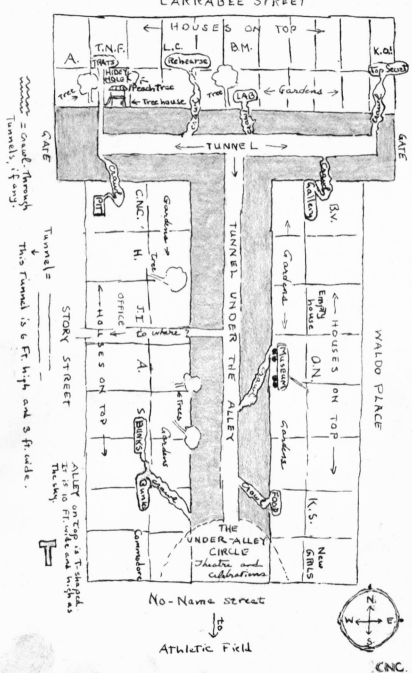

Chapter 1

Me and Tornid—Who We Are

My real name is Nicky—Nicholas Carroll. I don't like the name "Nicky," so I have renamed myself—Copin. A fake name. The real name of my pal is Timmy—Timmy Fabian. But we have renamed him Tornid. Fake name also. Few people know these names. I am eleven, in Grade Six. Tornid is eight, in Grade Three.

In this Alley where we live in Brooklyn, there is nobody my age to pal around with and nobody Tornid's age for him. There is a strike on in school right now, no teachers there. Our school pals live too far away to come to the Alley to visit unless it's an overnight deal, and there are too many of us Carrolls to ask them to sleep over. No room. The same goes for the Fabian family. So it's lucky Tornid and me both live here to pal around together. It's the month of May. Tornid and me hope the strike won't be settled soon because we have a big plan going and need time to work it out.

There are plenty of girls here in this Alley, but Tornid and me don't count them. We have to keep all our affairs secret from them, all our business. "Contamination," we call the girls. Me and Tornid have to call the girls "Contamination" to keep them from digging our top secret plans. We say the girls have been contaminated by fall-out. Or, by just being girls. We close our eyes, try not to touch them or brush up against them, hold our breath, keep them out of Connie Ives's kitchen—one of our head-

3

quarters—keep our mouths shut, and get past them, away from them as fast as possible. They don't like it, and the parents don't like it. But the game was not invented for them to like.

This Alley where we live—on the campus of Grandby College—is a T-shaped one with twenty-seven little houses on the three sides of it. All have gardens behind them backing onto the Alley, which has two gates—iron grill—one at each end of the top of the T and usually kept locked. This Alley is a good place to live. But it is the alley under the Alley that has begun to bug Tornid and me.

A boy named Hugsy Goode, who used to live in the Alley, said one time, "There are tunnels under these houses, and they go from house to house."

Almost all the time our plans, our maps, our drawings, our talk—Tornid's and mine—are about that alley under the ground. Even though afterwards Hugsy Goode said it probably wasn't so, we—Tornid and me—we believe it. We believe in the underground alley. We draw mazes of it, we inhabit it with good people and bad people, we have wars between two sides down there, in their bunks, their depots, their pits—we map out the areas of all their businesses down there. We have a lot of time for all this now because of the strike.

This book is about that underground alley.

The main people that are going to be in this book are Tornid Fabian, my pal, and me, Copin Carroll. Forget the "Timmy" and "Nicky" names our families know us by. But don't say, "Who's that?" if one of the moms calls us by those names as the book goes on, because they don't know our aliases. Not yet, anyway. Remember:

Nicholas Carroll or, ugh, "Nicky" = Copin Nubsy Carroll
and
Timothy Hill Fabian or "Timmy" = Tornid Nubsy Fabian.

We have adopted the same middle name as part of our aliases.

There are six of us Carrolls now. My mom and dad stick to Christmas names, on account of Carroll, in naming us. So the two youngest are Holly, aged three—a real ham—and Branch, a boy of one-half, real neat so far. The names of the others of us are: Steve, my brother, aged fourteen, real pious and residing on the other side of this room where I'm writing now (He has the best view of the Myrtle Avenue El.); Star (ugh) *contamination,* aged twelve; then me, Copin, aged eleven; then Notesy (ugh) more contamination, aged nine. You could say Holly and Branch start a new line of Carrolls, the rest of us being semigrown.

Now take the five Fabians, from the top. There is Isabel (ugh)—*"Contamination* Blue-Eyes" we call her—aged ten; next, aged nine, comes (ugh) Beatrice—*"Contamination* Black-Eyes" we call her; next comes my pal, Tornid, eight; next Danny, aged six, a busy boy; and last, Bill, aged four, who prints his name LLIB—Bill, spelled backward. It isn't that he spells his name backward on purpose. It is that he starts the "B" so far over on the right-hand side of the paper he has to put the "I" to the left of the "B" and so on. So it comes out LLIB. His mom says he will outgrow it, he is only four—says Danny used to do the same. Too bad, because LLIB looks neat, like code. Contamination Black-Eyes should try to stop trying to reform him. YNNAD would look neat, too, in our code.

Now you know the main people who are going to keep coming in and going out of this book. Some other people who live in this Alley may come into this book now and then, because there are twenty-seven families here and most people know everybody, or at least have their number. But this chapter is not meant to be a who's who of the Alley. And I'll tell you who the people are when they creep in, whosoever or whatsoever they may be—I know not yet myself—as we get on into the top secret affair of the tunnel under the Alley.

The people who used to run things in this Alley have gone off to college—Connie Ives for one. When she comes back, she says "Hello" and has a conversation with me and Tornid. A neat girl, too old to classify as *contamination.* Billy Maloon—solver with Connie of a burglary they had in the Alley long ago—he's in college now, too, and has grown a beard; Arnold, the Rapid Advancement boy, in college and grown a beard; Hugsy Goode, thinker-up of the tunnel under the Alley—he's in college now, too, and grown a beard; Katy Starr, the law-maker, the Arps, all, all in college now. Gone.

It is me and Tornid, now, in charge of the affairs of the Alley, now.

The Fabians have a dog, Sasha, a golden afghan; they also have cats, fish, birds. Whatever comes their way, "Come in, come in," they say. Animal-loving people. Not *my* mom. Once we had one cat—*one*—named J.C. He went away long ago. We have had none since, though my mom permits collecting worms and butterflies.

And now, I will tell you the really sad news about the Alley. Talk about no place to go! We *used* to have a Circle at the end of the Alley to play in, to have a game of ball in, to turn our bikes around in. No more. No sirree. It is disgusting to have to relate that it was blasted away one spring day three years ago when I was eight and Tornid five. The four families whose yards backed onto the Circle wanted more garden. Each family gobbled up part of the Circle and attached it to their yard.

"Is this democracy?" my sister Star shouted.

No use. On went the blasting, the four families didn't care . . . they didn't have any children any more. Now, the Circle end of the Alley looks like a concentration camp, and I heard a Gregory Avenue kid looking in on Tornid and me one day say, "The poor kids, they have to stay in *there?*"

Yop. Now . . . no place to turn around in, no place to play games . . . the Circle, headquarters for all the life of the Alley . . . gone.

That is the reason Tornid and me have to think more and more about the tunnel that Hugsy Goode said probably exists under the Alley. Some place to go to make up for the loss of the Circle. You have to have some fun. The underground alley will belong to all, and we, Tornid and me, will be in charge. Let those families on top of the Alley try to tear down the Circle of the alley underneath —if there *is* a Circle down there—and see what happens. Just let them. Hah!

"Right, Torny, old boy, old boy?" I said to my pal. Tornid and me were sitting on the curb of where the Circle used to be.

"Right," said Tornid.

He has ESP and knows my thoughts.

Chapter 2

Tunnel—Top Secret

Tornid and all the Fabians—pets, dogs, fish, birds—live in the important house in the Alley where Hugsy Goode used to live, the guy who said there might be an alley under the Alley. This house has a hidey hole under the dining-room windows, and the hidey hole has two windows of its own that look down into the Fabian cellar. You can't see in or out of those windows, though, because they are covered with squash vines that Hugsy Goode planted long ago. The whole hidey hole is covered with these vines, and if you are down there under the thicket and don't rustle the vines, no one knows you're there.

It's lucky that my pal Tornid and all his family were the ones who passed the stiff specifications of Grandby College and were allowed to occupy this particular house. Because its hidey hole is where Tornid and me think up ideas about the under alley. Then we go over to Jane Ives's house, draw up the maps and plans, sometimes labyrinths, and store them under Jane's television.

Jane Ives is Connie Ives's mother. I call her "Jane." Tornid calls her "Mrs. Ives." It's the custom in our house to call most mothers and fathers by their first names. In Tornid's, it's the otherwise custom—call them "Mr." or "Mrs."

Tornid and me go over to Jane's kitchen to get warm, to talk, to have a snack, maybe, and then to draw at the dining-room table. She lets us keep our things—paper and

9

plans and things, a ruler—under the television set, rarely, if ever, looked at in the home of Connie Ives. Only if there is a historic event. Then they look. Jane doesn't even know, never even heard of Bob Dylan . . . who he is. She does like the Beatles, though, unlike my mom who can't stand them. Jane lets me play my Beatle record on her record player. . . . I'm the only non-member of the Ives's household that may turn on her stereo . . . the only one. I wish someone would tell my mom that. And my dad. Jane knows about the tunnel, is in on the secret of our aliases, is sworn to secrecy.

At the front of the book I put one of the tunnel maps I drew, and I'll explain it here, so keep your finger on it.

The Alley on top is shaped like a capital T and always will be shaped that way even though the Circle, the best part of the Alley, has been removed—none of us can get over that—I don't care if I do harp. Tornid and me figure that the tunnel under the Alley will be shaped like a T, too, with offshoots, minor passages leading to various pits, and with a Circle, still intact—we hope—at the end.

Examine the chart. Find the main entrances or exits, whichever you want to call them, for the tour of the tunnel. First: there is the entrance through, we think, Tornid's hidey hole, marked T.N.F. for Tornid Nubsy Fabian. Next, under my house, the first house on Story Street, there is a pit, marked C.N.C. for Copin Nubsy Carroll. This pit is an office or a rendezvous with bunks stacked up to sleep in.

Come back to the main tunnel. Stop off for a while under the house of LLIB's friend, Lucy Crane (marked L.C.), where there is another office, we think, for food, or a place to rehearse plays or make plans to outwit smoog-men, if any, in the tunnel. Then proceed to the end of the top of the T, the opposite end from the Fabians' house and marked K.O. for "Keep Out." Stay there a while any-way if you want to study the Top Secret business that goes on there. Then come out and crawl—in most places we think the tunnel is wide and high enough to walk in, six feet high, three feet wide; but in others, it is a crawling tunnel, not to have monotony—so next you have to crawl through the bypass to the office—it might be a gallery—under Bully Vardeer's house, marked B.V. He is the artist of the Alley, paints everyone, and his house in the Alley is opposite us Carrolls.

Then come back from that office marked B.V., crawl back, that is, to the main tunnel and to the place under Billy Maloon's house (B.M. on the map). Above the tunnel here, there is a rain drain. This drain is always clogged up and creates floods outside the back stoops of the houses that face Larrabee Street, especially the Fabians' house, which is at the lowest part of the Alley. Of course the drain does not drain down into the tunnel. If it did . . . brother! Everybody would know about the tunnel then, be able to see down, see what was going on, and where would be the sense of the tunnel then?

Back to the map again. In the tunnel, from where the drain is on top, in the middle of the top part of the T, and in the main stand-up part of the T of the tunnel, you can look up the long end of the T to, we hope, the under-alley Circle. First, though, to the right, there will be a cutoff leading to the most important TOP SECRET OFFICE of the tunnel, under Jane Ives's house, marked J.I. The main business of all the businesses is conducted here, we think. What that business is—that is what we hope to find out. As fast as we are certain of any fact we'll pass it along to you. We have to consider why the tunnel is here at all —we have a dozen theories, new ones every day—and find out if it is used now, why and by whom . . . or what?

Opposite J.I.'s house there is another pit for mechanical equipment . . . shaped, perhaps, like an old trolley car. It is under the house of Orville Nagel, an expert on old train whistles and signs and a collector of trophies from torn-down els and retired subway trains. Let's hope the Myrtle Avenue El will never be torn down and be the next to have a bit of it, a sign or a signal, just wind up in this neat man's house. He has red lights and green lights in his house at his front door . . . go . . . stop. His pit underneath is marked O.N., and when the tunnel is discovered, he will be a great help to fix it up for tours. We figure his pit is used for signaling and computing and sending top secret messages to the other pits. Then there is, at the end of the Alley, the pit marked K.S.—for Katy Starr —perhaps a library or a candy shop . . . a school, maybe . . . or a restaurant, a motel.

So far, all this is just guess work. It's a neat time of year to begin our questing . . . early in May. Days are long. There's no school. We can stay out later than usual without my mom blowing the cow horn, her newest noisemaker, for me to come in, or yelling, "Nick!" like the crack of a whip.

Chapter 3

Beginning of the Tunnel Quest

Now you have the lay of the land. Tornid and me are sitting on the big trash can outside of my yard waiting for a chance to collect tools . . . pick, shovel, whatever might come in handy . . . and get into Tornid's hidey hole to begin our excavations for the lost tunnel of the Alley. All the houses that face onto Larrabee Street have hidey holes. Tornid's is the best one and is historic, having been used as a jail in olden Alley days by the kids in charge then. Right now, we can't get past our moms who are hee-heeing and chewing the fat ("spewing" might be a better word) at the picnic table in our backyard, it being a lovely balmy day and the ninth of May.

We put the finishing touches on the shillelaghs we had carved for ourselves out of strong branches that tree trim-mers had cut off the big tree in Billy Maloon's yard. I put my initials C.N.C. on mine with a jackknife, Tornid put T.N.F. on his. We spit on them and polished them with sand and they were smooth. They are to be our staffs in the under alley.

"Why don't they go in?" I asked Tornid in disgust. "We have work to do."

"I dunno," said Tornid. "They like to talk." And he spit on his shillelagh.

At last, to throw the moms off the track so we could start on Operation Tunnel, I said in a very loud voice to Tornid, "So long. See ya." I gave him a wink that meant stand by in his yard and get whatever tools he could out of his cellar and hide them in the hidey hole while I tried to collect mine.

He gave me a wink, too, and said, "Bye. See ya."

I tore past the moms and up the stoop to the kitchen. My mom caught me up short. "Well-ll?" she said. I put on the brakes. "What are you up to now?" she said.

I kept my cool. "Social studies," I said as quick as a flash, forgetting there wasn't any school anyway.

This simple reply started the moms off on a new tack, and they didn't hear me go down into the cellar by way of the kitchen. I quietly assembled some tools . . . a small shovel, a small ax, a trowel, various chipping tools. That's one good thing about my mom. She has every possible tool . . . you name it, she has it. Even an adze.

Then, at last, it seemed the moms were breaking it up. I watched them through a crack in the bulkhead of the cellar door that opens up on the garden by the picnic table. At the same moment that Tornid's mom went out the back gate which squeaks and my mom came into our kitchen, I opened the bulkhead as quietly as I could and hid my tools under our honeysuckle, making sure the coast was clear. It was. Then I whistled softly, "It was a long day's night" (me and Tornid's usual signal), and I heard him whistle back. De dum-de dum dum dum-m. He came to my fence. I handed my tools over to him. We moved them all to the hidey hole and hid them under the squash vines.

"All set?" I said.

"All set," he said.

We adjourned temporarily to the tree house in the Fabians' yard to get the lay of the land, make sure we were not being watched. This was study time for some. School or not, we all had to keep up, and it was piano lesson time for Contamination Black-Eyes. She is the worst, the very worst, about not letting our least little move go unnoticed. Then, innocently (hah!) she brings it up when it will count the most, in front of a mom. She says, "Timmy. What were you and Nicky (that's us, remember) doing with shovels and things . . . where were you going with them? You know Mommy and Daddy don't like you to take the shovel out of the cellar . . . there's no snow to shovel . . . unless you ask. Did you ask?"

I said all that to Tornid.

"I know," he said gloomily, hating to have to say this about one of his very own sisters.

Well, luckily that Contamination girl was having her piano lesson. She takes from Lucy's mother, named Cornelia Crane, and was in there now; you could see the two of them through their dining-room windows in the house next door—Mrs. Crane and Contamination Black-Eyes, sitting side by side at the piano, arching their necks, bending their shoulders, like true musicians do. Every Fabian, except LLIB who is too little, takes piano from Lucy's mom, one of the nice moms. Lucy herself is too little to qualify for "contamination." There was no sign of the rest of the Contamination tribe.

This tree house of the Fabians is not a real tree house made out of boards and nails and constructed in a big tree. Couldn't be. The only tree in the Fabians' yard is a peach tree Hugsy Goode planted when he lived here, and it's in blossom now. This tree house is a bought metal tree house on top of high metal poles, and it has a red and white striped tin canopy over it to keep rain out. It has a ladder to get up onto it and a slide to slide down from it. It's a neat place to give shows and circuses on, or to just plain sit and think, or to watch what's going on. LLIB and Lucy often give a circus on it and have their lunch there, even in the rain.

Anyway, right now, nothing was going on anywhere that we could see, which was good for us. Because what was about to be going on was going to be done by us . . . Tornid Nubsy Fabian and Copin Nubsy Carroll . . . at the start of historic excavations.

We slid down the slide, hurried to the hidey hole, lowered ourselves into it, checked our apparatus, felt the walls. They were made of brick, dark red brick, like the houses, and were covered with dried vine roots and twining thicker branches. The wall behind us was just plain wall, as were the walls to our left and right. But the wall toward the dining room had the two small cellar windows above the Fabians' washtubs that looked out on the hidey hole. But they were so dirty and vine-covered we felt safe from snooping eyes, those of the Contamination girls, especially, who otherwise might watch us from the cellar while we worked.

We trailed some more of the squash vines over the windows and felt really out of sight.

The wall we were most interested in was the one to our left under the kitchen. We felt all along this wall to see if there was a door, a trap door, maybe, gone unnoticed all these years. There wasn't. With a piece of chalk I drew a large circle on this wall where I supposed the best place to begin the chipping should be, at the very bottom of the hidey hole.

On one side of the circle I wrote my initials, C.N.C., on the other, Tornid's—T.N.F. Inside the circle I wrote the word TRATS . . . our code word for START. Sometimes our code names are the real word spelled backward. We got it from LLIB . . . lucky he can't read. Too bad he and YNNAD (Danny) can't be in on all this. But they can't. I got out my map, studied it a second, put it back in my pocket. Each of us took out his hammer and chisel and . . . one, two, three . . . we chipped our first chip.

"Hooray! We're on our way!" I said to Tornid.

Tornid beamed. He has great gray eyes, always shining. Sometimes, Tornid wishes he was eleven or that I was eight. Most of the time we don't think of the age gap, we have so much to do.

We felt far, far away from the folks above. We felt we had already penetrated the secret of the tunnel and had left the lilac-scented air of the upper Alley for we knew not what sort of air in the under one.

Happily, we chipped another chip. Some flew against my eyeglasses. Lucky I wear nonshatterable eyeglasses. That's one good thing about my mom, she always buys the best possible eyeglasses . . . and lamps.

Just then, the sound of many voices . . . up above, not down below.

"Lay low," I said to Tornid.

We both lay low and listened.

What it sounded like, it sounded like the entire Alley population streaming into the Fabian yard. I got the gist right away. LLIB and Lucy, top performers in the tree house, were about to put on another circus. Perhaps some of the Contamination girls were also going to do an act. And we, trapped in the hidey hole at the point marked TRATS!

When the show started, it began with a performance, solo, by LLIB. He is known by some as the boy belly dancer because he has a certain knack. He can make his belly go round and round . . . revolve . . . clockwise and counterclockwise. No one else in his family can do this. Even though Tornid has a larger belly, he can't do this. So, now, LLIB revolved his belly.

After that solo, we could tell from the sound, the next act was LLIB and Lucy impersonating Tornid's and my mom. They gave a very good imitation of the sounds the moms make while sitting at the picnic table. We hoped that would be all and the audience would leave. But it wasn't. Contamination Blue-Eyes gave her magic tricks, and this took a long time because sometimes she had to look one up in her book and do it over.

Our two moms were sitting very close to the hidey hole. They had balanced their coffee cups . . . we could see through the vines . . . on a huge pipe, covered with a flat slab. Must be about sixteen inches in diameter and may have some meaning in connection with the under alley . . . we don't know yet.

It was pretty hot down here in our hidey hole. Tornid and me sure were glad when they got to the last performance. It was Danny, and he doesn't care much about performing . . . he told a joke. "Who is the father of all corn?" he asked. And in a second he answered himself. "POP corn."

And that ended the circus. Applauding loudly, everybody left . . . no lemonade and cookies, at least. So we picked up our chisels and chipped off another chip. The bricks were old and soft. "It shouldn't take very long to get through," I said to Tornid.

"I know . . ." he said.

Just then . . . I knew it . . . the cow horn . . . plus a bellow of my name . . . "Nick!"

We had to go in.

"Anyway," I said, "tomorrow is Saturday. Most people sleep late. But we can get up early and begin and . . ."

"And?" asked Tornid.

"*¿Quién sabe?*" I said . . . an expression I had learned in Mexico one year we spent there.

"*¿Quién sabe?*" Tornid repeated. We covered our tools with a big green plastic bag, in case of rain, and went home to dinner.

Chapter 4

The Glooms

Next morning Tornid and me were sitting under Jane Ives's rose of Sharon tree. It was Saturday, about ten o'clock. By this time we had expected to have gotten through the hidey hole wall. Instead, here we sit under the tree looking up through its new green leaves to the blue sky above. Why?

Two letters came to my house in the mail this morning. Both were about me. No wonder I have the glooms. One was from the Commodore—he lives in the end house on Story Street, one of the four houses where the Circle used to be. The Commodore is in charge of all the grounds of the campus including the Alley and its twenty-seven houses. Although he mentioned only Tornid and me by name, he said his letter was for the whole family and that he was also sending one to all twenty-seven families in the Alley.

The Commodore said: Keep our yards clean, keep toys out of the Alley, don't stick them in drains and then complain of floods, bring our bikes into our yards, especially the days the sanitation men come . . . or else the men, who were sick and tired of moving them out of the way, would just plain run over them.

The unfairness of mentioning me by name in this letter is what bugs me. When I was little, I used to help the trash collectors. I used to get kiddy cars and other toys out of the way for them and helped carry the trash cans to the big

21

truck. They all knew me and they thanked me in those olden days. Nowadays you don't have any little ones with the ambition to grow up to be trash collectors. They *should* be taught about their toys.

In the olden days there were laws in the Alley. They were made up by Katy Starr and called Katy's laws. Now —none. Dogs are allowed to roam up and down the Alley. Is it any wonder that the Commodore writes? But why does the Commodore pick me and Tornid out to name? True, Tornid and me did climb into the empty house next to the one marked O.N. on the map. We entered by way of the dining-room window . . . I am good at this and once helped a vice-president into his dining room that way. The painters had locked him out . . . don't ask me why.

We, Tornid and me, wanted to see if there was a door in that cellar leading into a pit of the tunnel. There wasn't, and we came back out in a hurry, worried because we didn't know whether smoogmen, one of our names for under-alley people if there are any, might be able to see through solid and be watching us. We had not done any harm—went in, came out, that's all.

Now the Commodore says he'll have all these twenty-seven houses mowed down, carted off brick by brick, the way they did the Waldo Avenue little houses opposite the Alley houses, if people didn't shovel their snow, stay out of empty houses . . . me and Tornid, specif . . . rake their leaves, stop letting their dogs out in the Alley, bring in their bikes and so forth . . . stop clogging the drains, stay out of where we're not supposed to be.

All that's fair enough. But what's it got to do with Tornid and me right now so's we have to sit here under the rose of Sharon tree and think gloomy thoughts instead of going on with the real work of this book . . . finding the tunnel? Because at ten o'clock . . . ten minutes to go

. . . Tornid and me, since we had the honor of being singled out, have to clean the Fabians' backyard and . . . with a dog like Sasha! Yechh!

And then there's the other letter that came. Yep. School. It was to my mom and dad. The strike doesn't seem to affect the letter writers there. It said, "Your son, Nicholas (yechh) shows poor comprehension in social studies. On a test that is given all over the country, we asked a simple question based on his textbook: 'And where is Mr. Lee taking you today, class?' Your son answered, 'He lost me on the banks of the Amazon.' We prefer to think this reply is due to poor comprehension rather than to a flippant attitude to social studies. It is a Mr. Jenks who, in the book, is taking two boys up the Amazon, whereas Mr. Lee, the man we were talking about, is on the Yangtze. Please come with your son to the principal's office on Monday."

"I never had a letter from school so far," said Tornid.

At home, he could be proud of this record. With me, he had his doubts.

I said, "You are only in Grade Three."

Tornid doesn't like school any more either. He had half-way liked school until I got aholt of him and showed him how awful it is—and what a waste of time! Well, Tornid will learn . . . it just seeps in gradually how awful school is. And that it gets worse each year. Yep. Each year worse than the one before, he'll find out. At least, I haven't as far to go to wind up the whole thing as he does.

Tornid sighed. "I wisht I was eleven instead of eight, so I'd be nearer the finish . . ."

I said, "You have to study hard, get yourself into the Rapid Advancement class, then you're in for the windup sooner."

For a minute we gloomed in silence. Into my glooming thoughts came the sound of the Myrtle Avenue El. To me it said, "Come on, Copin."

I said it out loud . . . "Come on, Copin. Come on, Copin."

"What?" Tornid said.

Sometimes I think Tornid only hears *me,* nothing else. "Listen, you cluck, listen to the train," I said.

Tornid doesn't mind when I call him "cluck" or "dumb cluck" any more. Likes it, in fact. He used to say, "I'm not a dumb cluck." And when I said, "I know it," he'd laugh his funny crackly laugh. He had gotten it straightened out that "dumb cluck" doesn't mean "dumb cluck" when I say it to him. It means "nice guy" and that he is my pal.

"Listen to what?" he said. "The . . . El . . . ?"

"Yes," I said. "The El. The Myrtle Avenue El. There it goes up the tracks with no Mr. Lee or Mr. Jenks to explain the sights."

Tornid laughed again. I looked at him piercingly

through my nonshatterable eyeglasses. If I'm gloomy, he's gloomy. That's the rule and no laughing. I said sternly, "There isn't any fun here in the Alley any more."

"I know," Tornid said. "Circle gone . . ." He looked at me to see if he'd hit it right.

I nodded. "Yeah," I said. "The Circle was free. It made you make up games. 'Here I am,' said Circle. 'Think something up.' "

"Could Circle talk?" asked Tornid.

I looked at him piercingly again.

"Oh, yeah," he said. "Like . . . smoogmen . . . I guess."

I heard another El. "Take the Myrtle Avenue El," I said. "This El on Myrtle Avenue is part of the last one in the entire city of New York. It begins at Jay Street and runs way out—maybe to Montauk Point for all I know. They used to run all over the place . . . els did. There even used to be one that ran across where the Mall is before there was a Mall on the campus . . ."

"Like there used to be a tunnel under the Alley and we're going to find it."

"Can't find it today because of the letters. . . . Clean up your yard . . . yechh. All those els are gone now, Tornid, except that one over there, running now on Myrtle Avenue . . ."

"Yeah," said Tornid. He was real gloomy now, too. "Maybe our tunnel won't be there, either. Gone like the El on the Mall . . ." he said. "And the Circle in the Alley . . ."

Another El came rumbling along. We couldn't see it from under the rose of Sharon tree, but we could hear it, hear them all . . .

"I never been on an el," said Tornid.

"Neither have I," I said. "Born here, under the shadow

of it, hear it chug along every day and night of my life
. . . three years older than you, Tornid—but neither
have I ever been on it."

"Wow!" said Tornid.

"And besides the El," I said, "there are lots of interest-
ing things to see on Myrtle Avenue itself. But we just plain
can't go over there. Only on Sundays, me and Star, or
Steve, can go over to Myrtle and get the Sunday *Times*.
That's all . . . go over, come right back. You and me,
Tornid, we can't go. *We,* that is, *I* am not trustworthy."

"Nowhere to go except down," said Tornid, trying to
remind me of something good in our lives . . . the tunnel.

I didn't feel like being cheered up. I gloomed some
more.

I thought. I'd really like to take Tornid over to Myrtle
Avenue, show him the sights over there . . . the junk
shop run by a blind man that students and just plain people
buy lots of neat things in, the old guy that sits in his
second-story window, wide open winter and summer . . .
looks like a Rembrandt etching, Jane Ives says, and he
does . . . I looked in a book. Never moves except to hurl
a curse . . . I won't say the words, they are in Italian
anyway . . . at someone down on the street who suddenly bugs him. Once I saw him spit out the window at
someone who only asked if she could come up and clean
up for him. And the old man spit. He said nothing. He just
spit out the window. Once he threw a pan of dishwater
down on somebody. People know to duck when they see
him in the window. Most do. Well, those are just a couple
of things to see. And above, you can watch the El come
rumbling along and go. It's a very cheerful train.

Oh, naturally, I . . . we . . . would never go over to
Myrtle Avenue with a five-dollar bill in my pocket, like

Hugsy Goode did once, I heard, and got robbed. No mother lets her kids go over to Myrtle with or without five dollars. I'd have more sense than to take five dollars over there . . . just one, maybe, one of my own dollars I earn from collecting newspapers from people in the Alley and tying them up and selling them to the Goodwill. I have about four dollars home, and I haven't put it in the bank yet. Some of this money is Tornid's, because he helps me and we are partners.

Along came another Myrtle Avenue El. "Come on, Copin. Come on, Copin . . ." it said to me. The sound of the El is cheerful . . . you like to hear it. In the sleet, in fog, in rain or sunshine, you like to hear it and see it.

Well, someday, a day like this one, a Saturday with forced suspending of tunnel work, I'd like to take Tornid over there to Myrtle Avenue . . . see the sights. By chance, I had a dollar in my pocket right now. I took it out. I showed it to Tornid. "This dollar," I said to Tornid, "is a marked dollar. The mark on it says, 'Spend me on Myrtle Avenue, Tornid and Copin.' Thank you, I said. 'You're welcome,' it said."

"A talking dollar?" said Tornid.

"Yep," I said. "Money talks . . . you've heard of that, even in Grade Three, you've heard of that. Right?"

"Oh, sure," he said.

"So . . . come on," I said in an offhand way as though we did this every day. "Time to get going over to Myrtle and spend this talking dollar, partly yours anyway, because you helped me collect and tie up the papers. We'll spend it, eat what we buy, sit on a step and watch the trains go rumbling by."

Tornid was silent. He is not used to doing things that are not allowed. None of the Fabians ever do anything wrong. Without benefit of blasts on the cow horn, my mom's rallying cry, whacks, awful looks, or sarcasm, the Fabians, each and every one of the five, always just naturally do what they are supposed to do. And have perfect manners, say thank you every minute. Bugs me why, sometimes.

Another little train came busily along. We had left the rose of Sharon tree and were standing now at the Alley gate where we could see it, a block away.

"What's that train saying, Tornid?" I asked.

"I dunno," he said.

"It says, 'Come on, Copin. Come on, Tornid.' That's what it is saying."

"Knows my name?" said Tornid. "My fake name?"

"Yes. But . . . the trains say something different to everybody," I said.

"Knows many languages?" said Tornid.

"Yep," I said. "And Spanish. Says, right now, says, '*Venite, Tornithos.*' Translated means, 'Come on, Tornid.' And it means . . . Now. Hurry!"

What won Tornid in the end was a song I made up on the spur of the moment, the tune and words based on some song I'd heard some time about something else. This was it:

> "Oh . . . the . . . good Myrtle Avenue Line
> It gets you there on time.
> Shake a leg, shake a leg,
> Shake a leg, shake a leg
> On the good Myrtle Avenue Line."

As I said, the song won Tornid. We climbed over the Alley gate . . . we are used to doing this and didn't tear our clothes on the barbed wire. Then we crawled under the iron gate at the end of Story Street. We were out and on our way to Myrtle Avenue!

Out of sight and out of earshot, we sang at the top of our lungs:

"Oh . . . the . . . good Myrtle Avenue Line
It makes you feel just fine.
Shake a leg, shake a leg,
Shake a leg, shake a leg
On . . . the . . . good Myrtle Avenue Line."

Chapter 5

The Good Myrtle Avenue Line

"Oh . . . it . . . gets you there on time . . . tum-te-tum, tum-te-tum, tum-te-tum, tum-te-tum . . . oh, the good Myrtle Avenue Line . . ."

Tornid and me felt fine. I bought some chewing gum . . . not allowed to have this—"Rot your teeth," says my mom . . . and a candy bar each in the little store where Star and me, or Steve, buy the Sunday *Times*. I got seventy cents back, two dimes and a Kennedy fifty-cent piece, which was good luck—there aren't many of them around—and bad, because I would not want to spend it. One side of it would say "save me," the other "spend me."

We went down on Myrtle to the corner of George Street where there is a closed-up shoe-shop store, and we sat on its stoop. In the window there were some dusty, high-heeled, pointed-toed ladies' shoes and one enormous pair of a man's black shoes size about eighty. We ate our candy bars. We don't have the knack that Contamination Blue-Eyes does of making a piece of candy last nearly all day, making everybody's mouth water. Yechh!

Across the street was that ancient man sitting in his small square open window on the second floor looking down on Myrtle. Nearby was a spooky-looking store front, covered with dusty brown curtains and a sign that said, "Come in. Mother Fatima will help you." There was a dusty stuffed pigeon in front of the brown curtains and dusty pale blue wax flowers. Looking up the other way, far,

far up the tracks, we could see a little train, and soon it would come.

"Next tunnel picture I draw will contain an offshoot from our Alley tunnel to this point here. Then, when me and you have completed our excavations, we can come over here often, even take a ride on the El, return by tunnel, and no one know we been gone," I said.

"Neat," said Tornid.

I counted my money behind Tornid's back, so no wise guy could see me. I had seventy cents left. I put the Kennedy fifty-cent piece back in my pocket and kept the two dimes in the palm of my hand, the price of a token. That's what it costs now anyway . . . hope they haven't jumped the price yet. They're talking about doing that, up it to thirty cents. Another good reason for taking our ride now, while it doesn't cost as much. The train was coming nearer, a few people were running up the stairs, not to miss it, the street was vibrating, the train was saying, "Come on, Copin . . ." I grabbed Tornid's hand . . . we joined the other people rushing up the stairs. I bought a token at the booth, shoved Tornid under the turnstile. I dropped my token in the slot, and we were on the platform in time to see the Myrtle Avenue El sway into the station. The whole place shook and vibrated and maybe would fall down before the guys had a chance to tear it down.

The train stopped. "Hurry," I said to Tornid. "We don't want to miss our train," I said, as though we took it every day. The doors opened, we stepped in, the conductor looked up the platform and down the platform, signaled, the doors closed. We raced to the front car and stood at the front door with a view down the tracks. The ancient man, below us now, was still at his window, and he didn't look up at the train as we went by, just waited for his enemies.

My first ride on the Myrtle Avenue El! At last! Wait till I tell Jane Ives! The train started up smoothly. There was only one other person in our car. She sat at the back reading a newspaper instead of looking at the sights. I thought she couldn't hear me, so I sang my song, "Oh, the good Myrtle Avenue Line . . ."

"Sing," I said to Tornid.

He said, "I don't sing on els."

Then I sang, "It's a long day's night . . ." Can't see why my mom doesn't like the Beatles . . . only likes Bach. De-dum-de-dum-m-m . . . dum-m-m dum. . . . Was I happy!

Tornid looked up at me and smiled. His eyes were shining.

"This is something like, eh, Torny, old boy, old boy?" I moved over a little not to hog the entire best spot in the middle of the front door.

"I can see all right," he said.

But I pulled him over a little anyway so he could see better.

And that's the way we went, the entire way down to the end of the line . . . the Jay Street station to be exact. The engineer came out of his cab here, walked through the cars to the back of the train with all his equipment, and got into that cab there. The back was going to be the front now. So we followed right after him. The conductor gave us a thoughtful stare, but he did not look unfriendly. We hoped he would not make us get off and have to pay another fare. All he said was, "Where you two fellas going?" I said, "Back to the George Street station where we got on." And (this shows how many nice guys there are left in the world) he said, "OK."

He picked up some newspapers people who litter had littered, folded them neatly, picked the best one, sat down, and read it. At last we switched over to the other track and started back. We were the only ones making the round trip. It was real neat when another train, coming the other way, came swinging and swaying along. When we passed, each engineer gave the other a toot and a slow wave of the hand.

When we got to the George Street station, Tornid said, "Come on, Copin. We have to get off."

"Cluck!" I said. "Now we have to go to the end of the line the other way, see what it's like up there . . ."

"I wisht I'd asked my mom or my dad," said Tornid, and looked longingly back at the station left behind.

"Too late now," I said.

The conductor came in, and he sat down in a corner of our car, getting up only at stations. He seemed to have forgotten about us and George Street. He opened up his paper and started to do a crossword puzzle someone else had begun on. I could see this because he was reflected in the window in front of us. If he asked me for a word, it might be "adze" because that is in most crossword puzzles.

It was much farther to the end of the line in this direction than the other. But it was a good ride. Pigeons were being exercised on the rooftops. On one windowsill a white cock crowed when we went by. Now, that was unusual. To the left, far away, we could see the Empire State Building and once in a while glimpsed the East River, so we knew we were still in New York City, though we weren't sure we were in the part of it named Brooklyn.

I wondered if we had been missed and whether someone else had cleaned up the Fabians' yard or if it were being saved for us. Well . . . guess where we finally ended up, where the end of the line was? In the middle of a cemetery that stretched as far as eye could see on both sides of the station. It was not a pretty cemetery. If you ever have a chance to ride the Myrtle Avenue El, go the other way, not this.

Finally, back down the tracks, homeward bound we went. I began to sing again and also danced a few steps of the frug. Tornid pulled at my arm. He was embarrassed. "There's a person on the train now," he said. Sure enough. There was . . . another lady. I could tell—the way she was looking at me—she didn't like the look of me or my hair. So, I looked back at her over my nonshatterable eyeglasses with gold rims. I didn't like the look of her hair either, on the order of an upside-down Baltimore oriole nest. We turned our backs on the lady with the nest hair. I said, "Contamination," and we forgot about her and did not care about her. Anyway, Jane Ives likes my hair, says it is not too long, and in school the kids say I look like Oliver.

Now, on our left, once in a while between buildings, we could see the Williamsburgh Bank building. This has the largest four-faced clock on the top of it that there is in the whole world, according to John, Jane Ives's husband, and he's been almost everywhere. The clock said two-thirty. I couldn't believe my eyes.

"Tornid," I said. "What time is it by that clock up there?"

"Half-past two," said Tornid. "Wow!"

"Must have stopped," I said. "Must not be going."

"Yeah," said Tornid. "Because if it was half-past two, lunch would be over and we haven't had lunch."

Next view of the clock said two thirty-five. It had not stopped, and by now plans were probably being made for our punishments. I tried not to think about these . . . they'd be more than cleaning up the Fabians' yard, you can be sure . . . as we clickety-clacked our way down the tracks on the home stretch. Pigeons back in now, smells of bread being baked in the famous Italian bakery below where my mom buys pizzas, of Rockwell's chocolates, of coffee. This is the best ride I've ever been on in my entire life. I've never been to Disneyland and can't compare it with those rides. I bet they can't beat this ride there, though, and nobody should ever tear down this famous El . . . ever.

The next station was ours. We went to the door. I turned around and looked sternly at Nest-Hair and piercingly through my gold rim eyeglasses, pursed my lips together thoughtfully, and me and Tornid got off. Ready for come what, come may. "The wheels of fate grind slow, but they grind sure," I said. A saying of Mr. John Ives, a man of many sayings.

"That the name of this train . . . Fate?" asked Tornid.

"May be," I said.

Down on the street now. Nearly three o'clock. They would not expect us for lunch any more. They would have eaten up all the lunch.

"My legs wobble," said Tornid.

"Mine, too," I said. I bought each of us a hot dog from the man on the street, fifteen cents each without sauerkraut on them, and two orange drinks, ten cents each, and so the "spend me" side of the Kennedy half-dollar had won. Good-by to it, good-by to the El, hello punishments.

We sat down on the same stoop as before, and the antique shoes were still there. It seemed a year since we'd sat here before. I ate my hot dog in about three bites, before Tornid had even taken one. He did not seem hungry. I was putting off the come what, come may ordeal.

Suddenly Tornid yelled. "Hey! There they are, there's my daddy! There's the Pugeot!"

He was right. There they all were, car overflowing with brothers and sisters, his and mine. They were going slowly down the street, opposite us, arms stretching out on both sides of the car, calling, "Timmy, Timmy . . . Nick, Nick," to right and to left. They didn't see us because a bunch of men had come out of the bar next door and were standing right in front of us, arguing.

Tornid got up, ready to shout, race across the street, traffic light say go or not. I pulled him back down and clapped my hand over his mouth. "They'll hit you, you crazy?"

"I don't care," said Tornid, and threw his hot dog, litter or not, in the gutter.

"Cluck!" I said." I could have eaten that . . . wasting good money . . ."

"You said some of the money was mine, and I don't care anyway."

But he didn't cry. He's game, my pal Tornid is. There was a great silence after our families had gone around the corner. No train came rumbling by on top, and no trucks came roaring along . . . the light was red. In the silence, from far away, we heard the blast of my mom's cow horn again and again and again. It sounded like a ship in distress.

"You hear that?" asked Tornid.

"Of course I hear it, cluck!" I said. "And now we'll make a dash for home. Let's hope the moms are blasting off in the Alley and not out front on Story. Then I can sneak into my house and you can climb into your tree house, pretend that you are sound asleep, have been asleep all morning . . . you must have ate something, you can say, that put you to sleep, and what's all the fuss about . . . you can say . . ."

Suddenly, just as we were about to dart between stores into a passageway to Larrabee . . . "Stop! Timothy! Stop! Stay right there! Don't move an inch! You, too, Nicholas Carroll!" (Remember those are our real names, not our *top secret* aliases.)

The voice of Mr. Fabian. The angry, though quiet, voice of Mr. Frank F. Fabian. (I usually call him Frank but probably never will again.)

Come what, come may was on us now.

Chapter 6

The Homecoming

The voice of Mr. Frank F. Fabian, his stern and quiet voice, held us rooted to the spot upon which we stood. He stopped his car right where it was, and never mind the honking of the truck of the Seven Sabatini Brothers behind him, unable to pass, its driver shouting bad words. The arguers from the bar stopped their argument and tried to understand what the matter was. One shouted bad words back at the driver, thinking his swearing was aimed at him and shook his fist.

Like my dad, Mr. Fabian is a kind and gentle man. He did not say another word now, though, and his face was stone. He motioned us to get in. There was no thought of just beating it, running away. After Tornid, I got in. The brothers and the sisters were softly arguing as to which one of them had seen us first. Contamination Black-Eyes said. "I told you I saw them, behind those men. I told you so."

So, they had driven around the block, and sure enough Black-Eyes had been right, because we had been there, and now we were here in the Fabians' car. Everybody shut up once we were captured. They didn't look at us, either. They moved as far as possible to the other side of the car to avoid contact. You would have thought that me and Tornid were "Contamination," not the girls.

Silence shrouded us. Mr. Frank F. Fabian started up just as the Seven Sabatini Brothers truck driver managed to maneuver himself around us. As he came alongside, ready to hurl final outbursts of rage, even he shut up—when he sensed the pall—and drove off, jaw half open with some not-said last curse.

I'll quickly give the highlights of the homecoming.

Every member of the Alley including Jane Ives was on his front stoop or at his window. Mr. Fabian parked his car where he always does, way up Story Street beyond the Commodore's house. The Commodore was smoking his pipe and studying his new car and did not look up. We had to walk the gauntlet home in front of the porch standers and the behind-curtain watchers. No one said, "Hello." Jane Ives, seeing we were safe and sound, had gone inside before we got to her house.

We were marching in the middle of the street. Mr. Fabian held Tornid's hand tightly in his. I was walking alone ahead of them. The others of the rescue expedition walked way over to our left. They didn't want to look at the watchers. Some of our disgrace had rubbed off on them because they were related, and they walked with eyes lowered.

When we reached my house, the lineup changed—don't ask me why. We went up onto the sidewalk. Mr. Fabian dropped Tornid's hand. Tornid moved up beside me, us two notorious villains walking together again. But not for long. Tornid's mom, who'd been standing on our front porch with my mom, came to meet us. Now it was her turn to take the hand of Tornid Fabian. "I'll call the police and say forget it, they have been found," she said grimly to my mom as they marched past. Instead of going through our house and in their back way as they usually do, they unlocked the main gate and turned right on Larrabee to go in their own front door.

It had not struck me there'd be such a stir as this. All

I'd wanted was to give my pal Tornid and me a little treat, a ride on the Myrtle Ave El before they took it down, if they did. That's all. I had not meant to stay away this long. We hadn't run away, we hadn't been lost. I wanted to defend myself, but I could see there was no defense and, anyway, like in bad dreams, no words came out. It was a wonder I could walk.

Alone now, I made a sharp right turn into our front walk, went past my mom, standing there, cow horn in hand and saying nothing. No one took my hand. And no one gave me a swat either. I went inside.

"Where were you?" Holly whispered as though I were a grownup. It is her custom to speak to grownups only in whispers.

Inside the house everyone acted as though I wasn't

there. No one looked at me, no wallop came, no shouts of rage—unusual for my family, especially my mom. Holly continued to speak to everyone in whispers, though no outside grownup was there.

I went up to my room. Steve came up. He moved his things out to some vacant bunk in the attic where a student or visitors sometimes slept. I kicked the wall to show I didn't care. No one said to quit it. I quitted anyway. I lay down on my bed. The house was very quiet. The little trains came and went over on Myrtle. That was about the only sound I heard, and no one was squabbling with anyone.

At six o'clock, Steve brought me up a peanut butter sandwich and a dish of soup. He said he understood I was to stay in my room for an indefinite era of time, maybe a year, except for going to school when the strike got settled and coming home from it. He spoke in a singsong voice. He looked piously at me an instant, fluttered his light-lashed eyelids, and from the door he said Tornid was never to play with me again.

Later, my mom and my dad did come up to my room. They didn't wallop me, even then. They just talked to me. The gist was . . . and I knew it . . . that I had done wrong, especially to take Tornid off for such a long time and on such a trip without permission or even leaving a clue. Everyone had been in terror, and they were looking for a picture of us to give the police. They didn't know what had happened to us.

I knew I had done wrong. I was unable, still, to say anything. And they left. Since everyone was miles away from me, I threw myself down on my bed and cried. I wondered if even Jane Ives would hate me now, too. I thought of the tunnel. Now, when could Tornid and me find it? Had the trip on the Myrtle Avenue El been worth it?

I searched my mind for something to latch onto in this come what, come may time in my life. A little train came rumbling along. It sounded sad. It had grown foggy out. I looked at the little train, blurry lighted in the mist, and it looked pretty. As it chugged out of sight, a real neat plan got born in my head, something to latch onto in this come what, come may blight.

Next—the plan.

Chapter 7

The Plan

Save the Myrtle Avenue El. Make it a landmark.

That was the plan that got born in my head. According to Mr. John Ives who keeps up with everything . . . all Alley people, most of them, come to him for information about—you name it, anything!—they are talking of tearing down this El. I sat at my window and watched the Els go weaving through the mist in their businesslike way. It was as though they were saying, "Put in this—in your plan —put in that." So many ideas about the El were churning up my mind! I began to feel happy. You do feel happy when you have a plan and know it's a good one.

First I wrote the plan down, as the ideas came, not to forget any of it. Then I copied it carefully to send to the mayor. I don't think he and his landmarks people have thought of it, or Mr. John Ives would have heard about it and told everybody. Here's the plan, right hot from the brain, making the come what, come may blight bearable:

To His Honor, the Honorable Mayor of the City of New York, Mayor Woolsey
Gracie Mansion on the East River near 89th Street
New York, New York

Dear Mr. Mayor:

Here's my plan, my landmarks plan, about the Myrtle Avenue El in Brooklyn that I, I and my friend, Tornid, took a ride on today. It is the last El in New York includ-

43

ing Staten Island. There's more than one plan here really —any of them would be nice.

Plan 1. *Don't let them tear it down.* A rumor has been going around for years that this El is going to be torn down soon, the way all other elevateds have been. This would be a terrible mistake. People are very worried. How are they going to get from the cemetery out in Queens down to Jay Street, Brooklyn, to work or to shop at A. & S. in the morning and then back home again at night? Miss all the fun of the trip, day in, day out—people get to know each other waiting for the train, run if they hear it coming, and they like looking out the windows at the rooftops, like watching the pigeons flying there. Why not have it that this last El is proclaimed a *landmark?* A souvenir of bygone days? If you have never ridden on it, you should try to do that some day. You should see for yourself how nice this El is, especially if you stand at the front door and see the tracks ahead shining in the sunlight. In the rain, it would be nice, too. And in the snow and ice the wheels make sparklers on the tracks—a Fourth of July fireworks in January.

Plan 2. *A Feast Line.* If the day comes when you just have to say OK to those people that want to stop using the El as an el, you can still proclaim it a landmark, still not tear it down. You could do this:

Have it that each station is painted a different color. The people in each neighborhood could vote what color they'd like best. . . . I hope bright red would win for ours. And each station could be turned into a little restaurant up there, sky restaurants of the Myrtle Avenue El. And some, if people wanted, could have a small gallery connected, art or neighborhood items—odds and ends— strange garb like a Job Lots store, or a bookstore . . .

paperbacks . . . all kinds of books with book stalls outside in nice weather. The ticket booths could be where you pay for your food, or whatever you buy.

Each restaurant station could have its own food, specializing in the food of that neighborhood or of any special country . . . say, one Chinese, one Mexican, one Spanish, one Greek, one Italian, and so forth. You could get from one neighborhood sky restaurant to another by means of a little landmarks El train, also painted pretty colors. In the summer they could have open-air little trains, like at a fair. You could hold a competition and choose the best designs. I'm starting on some myself, tonight.

So far, no one but you, now, and me know about this plan. I'll tell Tornid Fabian and Jane Ives. They're my friends. That's all. They are in on all my plans. Tornid and me are trying to locate a lost tunnel we think exists under this Alley where we live on this campus of Grandby Institute. When we locate it, I'll let you in on that so you can scoop it and the Alley houses into the landmarks El bill, too. If you want to.

Your friend,
Copin Nubsy Carroll

P.S. My friend, with me on the ride today, Tornid Nubsy Fabian, lives at 1010 Larrabee Street.   C.N.C.

P.S.2 It could be the showplace of the nation, of the world, our Myrtle Ave El station restaurants could be. Expo El.   C.N.C.

After a while I made another copy of the letter for Tornid—to give him, if I ever see him again, even though he won't be able to read all the words yet.

I found a large manila envelope in my desk a magazine had come in, and I pasted a piece of paper over my name and printed the mayor's name and address on it in India ink. In the upper left-hand corner, the way the teacher says to do, I put my name, Copin Nubsy Carroll (using my fake name for luck), and my address. I hid all these things and went to bed.

Chapter 8

The Reunion

It's lucky that I had that plan and the tunnel plan to latch onto in my mind during the next ten days because the blight was pretty total. Get up, dress, have breakfast, clean teeth, do chores—empty trash, garbage, and such (Steve and Star are piling some of their chores on me, capitalizing on my disgrace)—go to school—strike's temporarily settled, thank goodness, so at least it's some place to go—come home, have snack, go up to my room, stay there until dinner. That was my life. Few words came my way, mainly sneers.

As for Tornid, I don't know whether he got a different variety of punishments than me since I didn't ask and no one volunteered the information. I acted like I didn't care, suits me fine, my life, and all that. I gave that impression.

Eventually I did hear. Trust Star to inform me in a roundabout way, saying to Notesy on the stairs, loudly so I'd hear, "I heard," she said, "that Timmy is never going to be allowed to play with Nick again, not even when he is allowed back out again."

"Not ever?" said Notesy. I could tell Notesy thought this was rough. She is the least contaminated of the Contamination girls, and I may drop calling her that. I'll tell Tornid to lay off of Notesy, that she's safe now. Not to hold his nose or shield his eyes when she comes our way. If I ever do see Tornid again.

How about our tunnel plans? He could dig somewhere and I could dig somewhere else, and we could meet underground if we charted the right course. But it's not as much fun to dig alone as with two.

Now. I still hadn't mailed my plan to the mayor because I didn't know whether it would take one or two or more stamps, and I wanted to show it to Jane Ives first, see how it struck her. So, one day I asked my mom . . . she was in a good mood, having coffee in the kitchen with Bayberry, one of Mrs. Fabian's nicknames, who lowered her blue eyes when I came into the room . . . I asked my mom if I could go over to Jane Ives's house a minute to look up something for school in her books.

I could hardly believe my ears. "Yes," my mom said. "Come back in half an hour. It's better than having you slam-banging up over our heads."

I went back up to my room and got my letter to the mayor, put it between the pages of a newspaper, and went out, not slamming the door in hopes of further reduction of repressions. I rang Jane's back doorbell.

She smiled. "Hey, Copin. Hello," she said. "I've sure missed you."

"Yeah . . ." I said.

Jane did not comment on the trouble I'd been in. We just picked up where we had left off ten days before. I carefully took my El plan out of the newspaper and showed it to her. It looked neat. Jane looked at the address, saw it was important, and washed her hands so they would not smell of onion.

"You're getting to be like John, writing letters to mayors and people," she said.

"Read it," I said.

She read it. She liked it. I could tell from her expression she really liked it. She was very enthusiastic. She said,

"It's great! Why hasn't anyone ever thought of this plan before?"

"How many stamps do you think it will take to mail it?" I asked.

"Well," she said. "I don't know. I'll mail it for you. I have to go to the Post Office anyway."

"I'll pay you back for the stamps," I said. "And don't tell anyone, not anyone at all, about my El plan. It's just as *top secret* as the tunnel maps and plans."

"OK," she said, and poured me some tomato juice that I fixed up with the usual Worcestershire sauce and salt and everything available.

Then I sat down at the dining-room table and consulted my maps and labyrinths and tunnel charts, dusty from their ten days' vacation under the television. But I missed Tornid, my partner.

"Seen Tornid?" I asked Jane.

"Haven't laid eyes on him in days," she said.

"Well, Jane," I said, "when him and me get back to

work and get the tunnel found, and if it does go on over to Myrtle . . . sometimes I think it does . . . and if the mayor *does* let the Feast Line be built, and galleries and restaurants in the stations, then maybe you and me and Tornid could go over there by way of tunnel on rainy days and have pizza or chow mein without your even getting your feet wet."

"That would be great," she said.

I started home. I was singing, "Oh, the good Myrtle Avenue Line . . ." but I stopped when I got close to home, not to remind the moms of that famous day and year.

Then . . . knock me flat!

When I got home . . . two pieces of news. One, I was going to be allowed out in the Alley again, but not out front. Two, Tornid was going to be allowed out, too, but not to play with me. Stunned at these tidings, I went back out and sat down on the curb. I didn't know what to do, release had been so sudden.

Then I went back in and got Tornid's copy of the mayor's letter. I put it in my pocket. If I had a chance, I'd slip it to him . . . if he came out.

Then I went back out and stood in the Alley and felt lonesome. Then I measured myself against the Arps' tree to see if I'd grown an inch in the ten days. I couldn't tell. Without someone's help you don't get an accurate report. Then I zinged a rope on the pavement to see dust fly and hear the zing.

I looked for Tornid out of the corner of my eye. Though we couldn't play with each other, I could mouth my words to him. Him and me often practice mouthing our words, not saying them out loud so Contamination girls could hear them. We always know what the other is saying. It is one of the things we practice, like sometimes speaking our own secret language, words we have made up. We have made a dictionary of these secret words, and of the code we use when we spell words backward like TRATS. We have many devices of keeping our plans, mainly our tunnel plans, top secret. They are all under the television in Jane Ives's house.

If I see Tornid out of the corner of my eye, I'll mouth real words, though, not made-up ones in case he's forgotten them in the ten days. I'll mouth, "Ya dumb cluck, ya . . ." so he'll know I don't hold it against him I'd gotten him in trouble. But . . . no sign of the guy. He might have died and people keeping it from me.

Then, my sister, Star! She came along, always the bearer of bad tidings. You have to sort them out, what to believe, what not. She said, "I hear Tornid is never going to come out in the Alley again. If he can't play with you . . . and he never can again . . . then he's going to just plain stay in. I caught a glimpse of him in the window," she said. "His face was so . . . white!"

Star wouldn't care if Tornid died. She'd be able to say I told you so to me till the end of my life. I hit the pavement with my rope, making it zing, and the dust flew up. And that was to show Star what was it to me. She walked off.

I thought, no wonder Tornid would rather stay in. If he couldn't play with me or even talk to me, and if I was out in the Alley, where was he going to be? The Alley isn't all that big to have non-speakers in it. Maybe I was selfish if I came out every day of the week and him feel he had to stay in. Maybe we should rig it up so's I'd be out, say Mondays, Wednesdays, and Fridays, and him be out Tuesdays, Thursdays, and Saturdays. We could split Sundays . . . me, morning, him afternoon, because he can't use Sunday morning because he goes to Sunday school, and I have to have Sunday second breakfast, usually sausage, at Jane's.

Then . . . knock me flat!

There came Tornid . . . walking slowly up the Alley. He looked bashful, and his shoulders were hunched over as though he thought all eyes were on him and he must shrink. I didn't know where to look or what to say, even in our silent mouthing-the-words language. I felt bashful, too. It's catching.

Anyway, out of the side of my mouth, I said menacingly, in plain straight-ahead English, "Get out of my sight, Tornid. Do you want to be incarsecrated again?"

"I won't be," he said. He looked at me straight on. He was still bashful, but he had spoken.

"How come?" I said.

"I dunno," he said. "They just said I can play with you in the Alley, or my house, or your house, or in Jane Ives's. That's all, not go anywhere. What's that you got there? Why's it so fancy? Is it about the tunnel? Another neat plan?"

"It's a neat plan, all right," I said. "But it's not about the tunnel. We get back on with that next."

I gave Tornid his copy of the El plan, which was named Cop. No. 2. "Read it," I said.

He just looked at it.

"Whatsa matter, cantcha read, ya dumb cluck?" I said. So we were friends like always and began to forget the ten days.

"I can only read my writing," Tornid said. "We're not up to this office business kind of writing in school yet."

"Listen, Torny old boy, old boy. This is a copy of a plan I have sent to the mayor. This is your own copy, your very own I made for you. I have the first draft of it that I made it up on," I said.

"Well, what does it say?" asked Tornid. "Is it very long?"

No contamination being around to eavesdrop, we climbed up the Arps' tree where the reading could be private. "Are you listening, Torny, old boy, old boy?"

"I'm paying attention," he said.

I read him the plan, addresses and all.

"Neat," he said.

"You're the co-author of this plan," I said. "Like you are the co-author of all my plans. Because you were with me the day I thought it up, the day of the famous ride."

Tornid laughed his crackly laugh. His eyes shone. "I never been a co-author before, not that I know of, anyway," he said. And he put his letter in his inside jacket pocket where it crinkled whenever he moved.

I looked at him solemnly. I said, "May this plan that I thought of that came out of that *in*famous journey, like the century plant that blooms but once in a century, blossom forth as beautifully and cancel out the disgrace of that day and year. How do you like that?" I asked. "I wrote those flowery words in an English essay last week for my English teacher, Miss Dinwiddie, a real neat teacher who wanted us to write something about what we'd been doing lately. Of course I didn't say it was a ride on the El . . . no sirree . . . I'm not letting anyone hear this plan until it is adopted by the landmarks association . . . if it is. For the teacher, I put the ride underground instead, a subway, and my plan for that was there'd be one special subway train, which you'd never know whether you'd get it or not, that would never stop and it would go and go and go to the end of the line and farther, way way out in the country where there are woods and plants and rivers. . . . She gave me an A, she did. Did I get a compliment from my mom? Nope. But then I didn't show it to her."

"I didn't make up any of that El plan," Tornid said. All Fabians have this streak of honesty.

"Nope. But you were with me, and I wouldn't have made it up if we hadn't gone. Right, Torny, old boy, old boy?"

"Right," he said.

Chapter 9

Tunnel Quest Resumed

The shackles on Tornid and me are untied now. By-gones, bygones. I can go to the library, to Mike's art store, and to school, except there isn't any school again right now. Strike . . . on again. Tornid has to stay in the Alley, but we have the three best houses to go in plus, with special permission, the house of Mr. Orville Nagel, the man with all the lights and trains and signs and souvenirs of parts of bygone trolley cars. His house is a museum. I wish you could see it. Neat! Sometimes he blows an ancient steam whistle from an Erie Canal boat for us. Neat! It's his front doorbell.

Tornid and me are standing in his backyard. We still feel strange, trying to pick up life where it left off eleven days ago . . . that would be seventy-seven days in the life of a cat, I'm told.

I said, "It's three days since Jane mailed the El plan. I haven't heard from the mayor yet."

"Maybe he lost it," said Tornid.

"Ya dumb cluck!" I said. "Mayors don't lose things. Jane Ives says he'll answer. And she should know! Says John Ives wrote the mayor once (he writes governors, senators, presidents, everybody all the time about anything that makes him rage), and it took the mayor two weeks to answer him. And he is a grownup. It always takes longer to answer a boy. I might not hear for a week, a month, a year . . . *¿Quién sabe?*"

"Sabe," said Tornid.

I said, "Ya know how long it took me to answer that chain letter I got from that guy out in Kalamazoo, Mich. 82089? One week. I had to copy it ten times and send it to ten different guys so I will get one hundred or more letters in the mail—how do you like that? I sent you one. It all cost me sixty cents in stamps. But I did it. If I hadn't a done it, someone, the last one—name was Pete Calahan —he could have cast a gloom on me and everyone ahead of us on the list. Now the mayor . . . he only has to write once, not ten times. Ya hear me?"

"Yeah," said Tornid, "I heard."

"One thing bugs me, though. Maybe I should have signed it 'Nicholas Carroll' not Copin. The postman has never heard of Copin. 'Whose that guy, Copin Carroll?' he might say to himself, and not leave the letter when the answer comes. If I see the postman, I'll tell him to watch out for a letter addressed to that guy, Copin Carroll . . . say he's my cousin from Omaha visiting here a while."

"Cousin Copin! Ha-ha," said Tornid.

"So now, Tornid, old boy, old boy. Back to tunnel work," I said. "We have to find the under alley before summer comes and all of us go our different ways. The teachers' strike is a gift from heaven."

We hopped down into the hidey hole. Vines had grown thicker since we started Operation T. (for tunnel) nearly two weeks ago. We were even more hidden now than then.

"I can't wait for the day when we'll find the main tunnel and then the cutoff one to the office under J.I.'s house," I said. I laughed. "We'll come out of it, find the trap door, or whatever kind of door it is, into her cellar, come up her cellar steps, smell the sausage from *that* side the kitchen door (we'll try to make it on a Sunday when she always has sausage), and say softly, not to scare her, 'Jane! Let us in. You went and locked the cellar door.' Hear her say, 'Why, Copin! Tornid! How'd you get down in my cellar when it's locked up tight?'

"Then I'd say, 'Stage 1 of Operation T. has been finished. Next stage, finding where the passage from your cellar leads . . . if it goes further than here . . . connects up with small passageways to different houses . . . is in the works.' Then, I'd invite her down to take a look around . . . take a little jaunt to where we began . . . right here at TRATS. So, back to work, ya lazy lug. The tools are OK. So, chip on, Torny, old boy, old boy, old boy. On to the tunnel! This tunnel exists all right. It's no pipe dream . . ."

"What's that . . . a pipe dream?" said Tornid.

"You don't know what a pipe dream is?" I said.

"Oh, yeah . . . sure," said Tornid. "You mean *pipe* dream, new way of getting into tunnels. . . . You use a pipe to do it."

"Hey," I said. "Your ESP might have sent you a message right then. You might have something there!"

"I might?" Tornid's eyes shone. He was proud to have "something."

"Maybe," I said, and looked at him piercingly through my nonshatterable glasses.

"It's best not to let people—Tornid—know when they —he—have—has hit on something, not to make them— him—conceited. Jane Ives works the other way around. She is all for praising. The least glimmer of an idea— "Great, great," she says even before it all gets out of your mouth (it's because she has ESP). Even some corny idea of LLIB's or one of the C. girls . . . "Great! Great!" she says.

In Tornid's and my combine it wouldn't work for me to

throw out praise. I have to be the one with the ideas. The combine just would not work otherwise. You can't have an eight-year-old having the ideas. Helper to carry out ideas—mine—OK. Have the ideas—his—no!

Well . . . Tornid . . . he knows it anyway when the idea he passes along to me is a good one because I mull over it. And that's all he cares about . . . he doesn't have to be told, "Great, great." He is an anonymous idea getter and giver. Of course, like with pipe dream, Tornid doesn't always know he has an idea. But I sure know one when I hear one. So I climbed out of the hidey hole a minute, and I looked at and studied the round pipe with the flat top on it that the moms set their coffee mugs on while they watch the baby, chew the fat, make each other laugh. I couldn't understand why it was there unless it was a pipe, a vent—perhaps—that was used to air out the tunnel. I marked it T.V. (Tunnel Vent). This would throw people—the C. girls—off the track because they —everyone—thinks those letters stand for television, not tunnel vent. But from up here there was no way of telling if this theory was right. We had to get down to prove it.

So, back into the hidey hole again then, me—Copin Nubsy Carroll—and Tornid—Tornid Nubsy Fabian— ready to probe the secret of the tunnel. We chipped away at the brick wall on the left-hand side of the hidey hole. It was hard work and it was hot work. In case you wonder what it was doing outside, it was being hot. We worked fast because I never know when my mom will blast the cow horn blast—she can blow various notes on it, for she is clever in the use of it—and blast me home.

"She always blows it at the worst time. Doesn't she— my mom—always blow the cow horn at the wrong time?" I asked Tornid.

"I dunno," he said. You could tell he was glad it wasn't his mom had the cow horn, but mine.

As we chipped away at the bricks in the miniature jungle of squash vines, I said, "Hugsy Goode was a prophet. He planted these vines that grow over this hidey hole. He spake the words that there is probably a tunnel under the Alley. This hidey hole that in olden Alley days was a jail is going to be the doorway into that tunnel."

"It is complicating," said Tornid. And he said, "Copin, why are we trying to find the tunnel? It's going to take up all our time."

I just stared at Tornid. I got out my map and studied it. He got out his. He was embarrassed he'd said a stupid thing. We scraped away some more with our chipping tools. A little hoppy toad hopped out and away.

I said, "Your mom . . . if she hears us chipping when

she's in the cellar . . . will think it is the return of that rat she saw once." And I said, "This is the way writers of history get the history they write, Tornid. They find bones, or something, and piece them together and name it whatever they think it is."

"Do you think we'll find *bones* down there in the tunnel? . . . Cripes!" said Tornid.

"Might," I said. "One day last year a bunch of kids were playing in the rubble where some old houses were being torn down—it was down near Brooklyn Bridge in the Heights. The workers had gone home, and these kids found a batch of skeletons, about forty of them. They left them intact and told the police. Now they're studying the whole bunch of them in museums. They think they might be colonists or Indians, they don't know which . . . redcoats, maybe. That was luck for you. Keep your fingers crossed . . . hope we have as good a break . . . even top the record. Who knows?"

"*¿Quién sabe?*" said Tornid.

Just then the cow horn did blow. "Told ya," I said. "Another minute and we might have made the breakthrough. The wall's feeling pretty crumbly now."

"Yeah," said Tornid. "I know."

We looked through the squash vines on top, to make sure we were not being seen by anybody. Then we climbed out, wiped the sweat from our faces, stashed away our tools, and emerged as the cow horn blew again.

Chapter 10

The Curious Visitor

This time the cow horn meant good news. My mom said . . . knock me flat . . . "How'd you like to have dinner at the Fabians' tonight?"

Where's the hitch, I wondered. But I said, "Sure. Did Bayberry (I thought I could begin to call Tornid's mom by her nickname since the glacier was receding), did she invite me?"

"Well, you don't think I did, do you?" my mom said.

Then Tornid came running over. "Mrs. Carroll," he said. "Can Cope . . . Nick . . . sleep over, too?"

"Who's Copenick?" my mom said. And she said, "Your mother must be out of her senses. You won't sleep . . . there might be school tomorrow . . . we won't know till late tonight. If there is, you'll be tired."

"Oh, we'll sleep, won't we, Torn . . . Timmy?"

So later, there I was then . . . knock me flat—I never thought it would happen again . . . at the dining-room table in the Fabians' home. This might make you think that Tornid's mom and dad had decided to forgive and forget the Myrtle Avenue El expedition. But I can tell that his mom is still wary of me. I hope someday she'll like me. I'm doing my best to make a good impression, stay seated, not hop up in the middle of the meal, not sprawl, not gulp down my milk or my water, use the right knife and fork and spoon—they lay them all out at each place, regardless of whether you're going to need the whole

61

shebang or not. It is to accustom you to the sight of
several forks and spoons. If you should go to a banquet,
you won't act like a clod and eat your salad with the
wrong fork . . . end up for dessert with the dinner one.

I'll give the lineup at the long table.

Tornid and me were sitting with our backs to the
windows above the hidey hole. LLIB (Llyeeb, I call him
. . . he likes it and I'm trying to get in good with all
Fabians, beginning at the lowliest), sitting on Tornid's
left and beside his mother, at the end of the table where
she can get to the kitchen if necessary; Danny on her left,
opposite LLIB; then the two C. girls—Beatrice, the black-
eyed C. girl (too bad she is opposite me because I don't
know where to look . . . you can't see into those great
black eyes); and next to her, Isabel, the blue-eyed C. girl;

and last, at the other end of the table is Tornid's kind dad, about to carve a little roast chicken.

Tornid and me have made our secret sign that temporarily makes us free from the Contamination, and we could even look into Black-Eyes' eyes without fear. I wish I could dig what goes on behind them. But I can't. I fare better with Blue-Eyes who may abide me better . . . I don't know.

Well, that makes eight of us at the dinner table, and the dinner was great. That's one good thing you can say about both the moms, they are wonderful cooks. Sasha, the golden afghan with a pedigree that goes back to Afghan the First, is nosing around under the table. There's a ledge that goes around under the top of the table. People sometimes stick their gum there, to save it . . . sometimes they forget it and it hardens and becomes part of the table, or Sasha gets it and chews it intelligently; or they put a piece of food on the ledge they don't like and don't want to tell their mom they didn't like it. Nobody wants to hurt Bayberry's feelings, and all kiss her when dinner is over and say thank you and it was good. So, Sasha gets a windfall now and then. But not from this dinner, as good as a Thanksgiving dinner and it's only May.

We were eating the dessert, which was apple pie. I had just a few more bites to go when . . . I don't know what made me—I *must,* like Jane Ives and Tornid, have ESP . . . I *felt* eyes on me from behind. I turned around. I saw a little animal looking in the window at us. "Raccoon" at first did not enter my mind, it was so unlikely. "Look at that cat!" I said. But the minute I said "cat" I knew it was a raccoon, though that's a hard thing to prove to some people, yechh.

C. girl Beatrice said, "It's not a cat. It's a raccoon."

"Raccoon!" we all said together.

The C. girls made a low-voiced comment. Since they are polite, they refrained from making a criticism of a visitor in their home, even though the visitor was me. But I could tell what the comment was . . . "Can't tell a raccoon from a cat . . ."

I do things faster than most people. I was the only one able to scoop up the last of my pie and, even so, be the first out the back door. But the raccoon had vanished in the misty May air. We searched for a while, though it was getting dark. Me and Tornid jumped in the hidey hole to keep the others from doing the same and came out saying loudly, "Nope, not down here." We didn't see him anywhere.

People who live in the country would not be astonished to see a raccoon looking in at them through a dining-room window. But it is an unusual thing to have happen in Brooklyn, especially the part I live in—the Alley on the campus of Grandby Institute, not near the zoo or anything.

My C. sister, Star, came out. She was jealous when she heard the news because she hadn't seen the raccoon. At first she said, "Aw, yeah . . ." to me, not believing. But the honest Fabian girls said, "Yes, Star. He really was here, looking at us through the window. Maybe he would have come in if we hadn't moved and if Sasha hadn't been there. He was bee-utiful!" Then Star believed. That is one advantage to being truth-telling like the Fabians. People get to believe you. They'll *never* believe that I meant "raccoon" once I'd said "cat."

LLIB said, "It's lucky it wasn't a skunk." Then he went into a long story which nobody listened to about how, once in Maine, Sasha chased a skunk and well, as I say, phewy! I tried to listen, though, being a visitor in their house.

We all went back in then, including Star, and we all had

another piece of pie. They make about five pies at a time there in that house . . . they have to.

"There now. That's all," said Bayberry. "You may all be excused."

That's what you do. In the Fabian house, you don't get up and leave the table one by one as you finish. You wait for everybody to finish, have their last bite, everybody turn their knives and forks in the right direction on the plate, not askew, helter-skelter on plate or table, everyone to press the corner of their napkin against their mouths, tap-tap, and fold them, not crumple them into a mess. Then everyone says, "Excuse me."

We did all this. Then we pushed back our chairs, and each Fabian child kissed the Fabian mom and said, "It was delicious, Mom." It is very nice in this home of the Fabians. No wonder the raccoon looked in longingly.

We took one last look out the dining-room windows and the back door. No sign of the strange visitor. So me and Tornid went to bed, not knowing whether there was going to be school or not tomorrow. Tornid slept in the top bunk. I slept in the bottom one, usually Danny's. Danny was sleeping in a spare bunk over LLIB's in the little back bedroom.

Tornid was out like a light. He always does this, goes out like a light, right when I am in the middle of a sentence, discussing the tunnel, maybe, or the El, or the unfairness of life—like them not keeping the swimming pool in the gymnasium open Saturday mornings during vacation time when you need it most, or the unfairness of the guards chasing *us,* who live here, off the Athletic Field . . . yechh. In all this interesting unfairness talk, Tornid goes off to sleep.

This bunk bed is hard. Danny may be used to it. But I'm not. How can Tornid just plain go off to sleep with this

new development . . . the raccoon, the Alley raccoon?
He was a beauty, well cared for. Not a mangy-looking lost
animal, which we would have liked, too, though. He was
spick-and-span . . . perhaps a student's pet that got
away from his dorm. We do have students here from faraway places. Might be a guy from Michigan like Pete Calahan, that guy I don't know that wrote to me anyway. Well,
what I'm wondering while I'm trying to get to sleep in this
hard bunk bed of Danny Fabian's is: Will the raccoon be a
help or a hindrance in the finding of the tunnel of Hugsy
Goode?

Chapter 11

Unexpected Help with Operation T.

Next morning . . . bad news . . . there *was* school. Tornid and me raced out of the house before breakfast to see if we could see the raccoon. Everyone else came out, too. "I dreamt he was in my bed," said LLIB.

"That was me," said Danny, "in the bunk above you."

We didn't see the raccoon, so we had breakfast and went to school. I had to race to get there on time and slid into my seat like a baseball player sliding to base as the last bell rang. "Slide, Kelly, slide," said my teacher. And we commenced the day.

My mom had replied to the letter from P.S. 2 this way. She apologized for my attitude about social studies. Apologized, too, for writing a letter instead of coming in herself in person. Said she'd tried but could never get into the school on account of the strike. Said Nicholas (me) was apt to think he was a wit. Said she was trying to curb this streak . . . we'd all work together . . . etc. My mom showed me the letter, her eyes agleam with her own wit in it. The letter was mild compared to what she said to me! And her voice she uses!

Anyway, the teachers with their strikes have more to think about than me and my "wit," and I am forgotten or forgiven ¿quién sabe? which. So in the S.S. book, Mr. Lee is taking us up the Yangtze River again, a review of that dismal trek. It was hard the first time up the river, and it's worse today after a "Hard Day's Night" in Danny's bunk. It's still the month of May. If only we could get on to something else! But the teacher says we have finished everything for the year and from now on until the end of June we are just going to go over and over and over everything we have had. Yechh!

Don't worry. I had the sense to bring my four by six brown spiral notebook with me that I'm writing this book in. Tornid said he'd write a chapter. Well, that's fair because he is my partner. "I'll get my works done Sunday," he said. "That's my homeworks day."

When I got home, all Fabians were already there—their mom picks them up in the Pugeot (quite a carload)—and they all had their snacks in hand. Tornid's mom makes up the Fabian snacks early. She puts cookies, or sugar-coated cereal, or little sandwiches, some surprise, in little plastic bags, one for each and all identical in contents. It's like Halloween trick or treat every day for all Fabians. We're not even allowed out, our family isn't, for trick or treat on Halloween. "Can't eat all that trash," says my mom. "Spoil your teeth."

Tornid gave me a nudge, and we sat down under the tree house, LLIB and Lucy being up in it having snacks, even though they don't go to school yet. Tornid slipped me a sheet of yellow-lined paper with words on it. He had done his chapter in school like I had because his teacher had not come to school, and they were sharing teachers there. A smart girl he knows there had helped him with the spelling. I read it—his works.

THE RACCOON

A RACCOON LOOKET IN THE WINDOW. IT WAS NITE. WE WERE EATING DINNER. I HAD A DRUMSTICK. WE LOOKET AT IT. IT LOOKT AT WE. IT WENT AWAY. WE DONTE NO WHERE

IT CAME FROM WE DONTE KNOW WHERE IT WENT. THE
GRILS DWONT NO ETHER BY TORNID FABIAN AGE 8.

"Very good," I said. "From now on we will call the
Contamination girls *grils*. It will be our secret name for
them."

"Right," said Tornid, and we turned to face the *grils*
eying us with suspicion from the Fabian back stoop while
eating their snacks . . . Black-Eyes' snack already gone,
Blue-Eyes still slowly eating hers.

Black-eyed *gril* had watched me reading Tornid's chap.
Her black eyes were larger and rounder and more secret
than ever. I closed my eyes . . . so did Tornid . . . to
avoid Contamination. But she put aside her resolve never
to speak to me again in her life (dinner, sleep-over, and
the raccoon last night making her think that I might still
be a guest in their house and had to be treated politely),
and this *gril* said, "Nick. We know where the raccoon'z nezt
iz."

(She is at a stage in life where she puts a "z" in a word
where an "s" is supposed to be. It's her game and may
have a meaning.)

Me and Tornid automatically made anti-Contamination
signs, held our breaths, closed eyes more tightly, covered
ears. But she stuck it out. She said, "Look up there in Mizz
Alderman'z tree. (Her house is the end one, next to—see
map—T.N.F., and has a big maple tree. Half the trunk
is in her yard and half in Fabian territory. Most of its
branches hang high up over the Fabians' yard.) "Way
up there, zee? You can zee a new nezt, large and blowzy,
built in a hurry, frezz green grape leavez, even zquazz
vinez, probably from the hidey hole, zome honeyzuckle
dripping over the edgez . . . up there . . . in the top-
mozt fork . . ."

Me and Tornid opened one eye each—the eye farthest from black-eyed *gril*—and looked up. Sure enough. She was right. There was a huge untidy, hastily built nest up there. We made the certain sign we make that temporarily expels Contamination danger and opened both eyes and uncovered our ears, breathed also. Then we had a good view of the nest. The raccoon had taken branches from all sorts of bushes or vines in the Alley, and it was very pretty.

"Oh, I knew it was there," I said. "I saw it this morning. Me and Tornid saw it . . ."

Tornid forgot that he is supposed to agree with me always, come what, come may, and he said, "No, we dittent, Copin. Beatrice saw it first—the minute we got home from school she spotted it . . . first." I stared at Tornid through my nonshatterable eyeglasses. He said, ". . . I think she did."

Black-eyed *gril* looked at Tornid with reproach in her non-see-through eyes. Blue-eyed *gril,* Izzy, sniffed. She shook her amber-colored ponytail—the way she was wearing her hair today—and both *grils* then joined LLIB and Lucy in the Fabian tree house where they—Blue-Eyes—could finish their snacks and watch the nest in hopes the raccoon would poke out his head or wave his striped tail.

Yechh! Me and Tornid couldn't get to our work in the hidey hole with *grils* in the tree house lookout. So we sat down under the raccoon's tree ourselves and became raccoon watchers, too. We didn't see him. Bird watchers watch and often there aren't any birds. To be a watcher of anything doesn't mean there always has to be any of that thing to be seen every minute; but you have to keep watching, in case. Then you say, "There it is!"

From the tree house came the words, "He'z probably azleep."

Black-eyed *gril* gave this information out to Blue-Eyes in a loud voice so I couldn't miss the message . . . that she had gone to the library and that she had found out in a book that raccoons sleep in the daytime. So he probably was asleep now, true to the habits of his kind.

Yechh, I thought. Thinks she's the only one goes to libraries! Tornid and me, we go to the Grandby Library to look up something, get permission to study old copies of *Popular Mechanics,* dusty and tied up in the basement, so we can make models of antique cars like the Rio, and we don't brag or mention the fact when we are sitting in the tree house, and we look up, besides, why worms come out of the sidewalk after a rain . . . yechh!

"Uh . . . *grils,*" I said to Tornid. "Forget them."

"Yeah . . ." said Tornid. "That's some nest that raccoon made up there, and he made it so fast . . ."

"Yeah . . ." I said. "Probably saw how we all liked being in a house, so he made himself one . . . homesick, probably for his old house, wherever that was . . ."

Tornid said, "I wish he was our pet. He's neat."

The two *grils* came down by way of the slide and sauntered down the Alley toward where the Circle used to be to see if two new girls (we don't know their names and we don't know yet whether they are *grils* or not— probably are) were going to come out.

Lucy and LLIB wandered off, too, so me and Tornid had the Fabian yard to ourselves at last. We hopped into the hidey hole to get on with Operation T. Summer would come and the breakthrough to the tunnel not made yet, what with all the interruptions—El trip, incarsecration, raccoon. There they are, listed in alphabetical and time-sequence order.

Down in the hidey hole . . . knock me flat! Yesterday we had been digging and we'd made a lot of headway at the place named TRATS. Today . . . I'm not kidding, the dug-out area was three times as large.

Tornid and me looked at each other. Who had made our crumbly place larger? Danny? LLIB? Had they been fussing with our tools? No, they were where we'd left them in the green rain-proof plastic wrapping. Had that sappy Bobo, the new dog of the Maloons, a digging type (he sure can make the dirt fly), had he been digging here? *Grils?*

How can anyone be sure about *grils?* While pretending they have no interest in anything we do, they probably, all the while, are dying to know exactly what Tornid's and my business is. While humming, seeming to be paying no attention to us, they probably are always taking us in, studying us, absorbing our ideas, because we have the best ones, to pass off as theirs.

Probably black-eyed *gril* had guessed, or perhaps even stolen, one of our tunnel plans from under Jane Ives's dusty television while incarsecration was going on. She probably wanted to be the first to set foot in the famous tunnel (we should name it after Hugsy Goode when we do discover it—all tunnels have names), the tunnel of the alley under the Alley, and then plant a *gril* flag there before we can plant ours. Black-eyed *gril* has to be the first to know everything. Now she wants a tunnel scoop. Yechh! Put it in the P.S. 2 paper.

"Tornid," I said. "If it *was* a *gril* that was down here digging next to TRATS, we have to jump out, run six times up and six times down the Alley to get the Contamination off . . . perhaps even take a bath . . ."

"Oh, no . . . not me," said Tornid. "No bath. It's not bath time, yet. . . . Hey . . ." he said.

"What?" I said.

"I bet it was the raccoon. . . . Hey, yeah . . . last night or this morning while we were at school . . ."

"Of course, ya cluck!" I said. "It was the raccoon. Had a very busy night, building a home and digging our diggings."

After I had implied that I'd had that raccoon idea first, I looked at Tornid through the lower part of my glasses and pursed my lips together. I said, "You may get to be a Rapid Advancement boy, like the *grils* are R.A. girls, when you get bigger . . . you have so much ESP."

Tornid laughed his funny husky laugh.

"There's more of a mystery here than we'd thought, Tornid," I said. "You don't get raccoons doing unusual things, digging around a place named TRATS where there is probably an opening into a lost tunnel. Perhaps he,

being a raccoon . . . raccoons are famous for their curiosity—your zizter (I imitated black-eyed *gril*) told uz that
—well, he may already know more about this tunnel than
you and me put together with all our ESP thrown in. Or,
he may be a something—a smoogman—in disguise. On
a mission from below, maybe, to find out who, or what, is
chipping into the T.N.F. office that we hope is down
there."

So we began to dig, claw, and chip away furiously with
our hands, shillelaghs, ice picks—all our tools—spurred
on by this unexpected helping hand of the raccoon's, be
he friend or be he smoogman foe. We longed for the breakthrough. "Where are Nicky and Timmy now?" the moms
would say. "Over at Myrtle Avenue again?" they'd say.
"Never fear, moms. We'll never do that again. Where we
are, there's no rule against it," we'd say. "Down in the tunnel of Hugsy Goode, moms, the alley under the Alley. If
Alley above is allowed, then so is alley below," we'd say.

Tornid and me laughed very hard at the idea of the
funny times lying ahead. But we're not down there yet, and
there's plenty to do. We should be nocturnal like raccoons
—we'd be down there by morning.

Just then Tornid's dad came to their back stoop and
called in his perfectly ordinary plain-speaking voice, the
way he always does, as though his children can hear him
though nowhere in sight, "Billy! Danny! Timmy! Come
get your hair cut." He cuts everybody's hair, the *grils'*,
too. My mom does ours. The moms have hair-cutting
shears they share, one of the good tools bought at Job
Lots.

We got out of the hidey hole in a hurry before LLIB and
Danny or anyone else could see us. "Try and save some
food," I told Tornid. "Tomorrow is T.N.F. day, and we
may need food. Ah . . . tomorrow! Nothing to be scared

of, Torny, old boy, old boy . . . nothing coming at us
. . . I hope . . ."

"No Minotaur," said Tornid, laughing

His mom is reading the Greek myths to them all before
bed . . . they always read at least an hour, all the
Fabians, the mom or the dad reads out loud . . . all on
the big bed in the front bedroom. Now it's Theseus, and
Tornid has gotten our maze plans and tunnel plans all
mixed up with the labyrinth on Crete where Theseus
sought the Minotaur. Tornid worries for fear that, once
down there, if the tunnel really turns out to be a complicated labyrinth instead, we'll never be able to get out.

"Don't worry," I said. "The way I have it figured, in
our maze or tunnel, whatever it turns out to be, there's a
way in and a way out." And Tornid went in to the hair-
cutting ceremony. Do you dig that? Everything is a ceremony in the Fabian house. I sat in the tree house a while
mulling this over, mulling over all our plans. Then I
jumped down and went in because the cow horn blew.

Chapter 12

On Our Way to Somewhere

Next day, no school again, another holiday for Tornid and me. Early in the morning I went over to Tornid's backyard and went up into the tree house. I looked up in Miss Alderman's tree for the raccoon. No sign of him. His nest was still there, but its vines were wilting and spilling out of the fork of the tree.

Tornid came out, said (he speaks in a monotone, no ups and downs), said Sasha had eaten his tunnel supplies he'd saved from dinner on the ledge under the dining-room table, part of a pork chop—it was tough—and part of a baked potato, mostly peel.

"The best part," I said. "Where are the *grils?*" I asked.

"I dunno," he said. "Maybe over at Jane Ives's," he said.

"Don't you think it's strange," I said, "that the *grils* haven't caught on to our work in the hidey hole? In and out of your house a dozen times a day while we are chipping and chiseling? How in the name of Sam Hill . . ."

"Who's he?" asked Tornid.

"A friend of John Ives," I said. "But I'll tell you why they haven't conned our top secret T. business. It's because they haven't opened the trap doors that seal their minds and let in the meaning of what's going on right under their noses. They have clues . . . like, where we are all the time . . . and they don't even know they have a clue.

Yes. Some people are like that. Now, you and me, Tornid, we know a clue when we read, hear, see, or guess one. We may even see more clues than there really are. But that is better than not seeing any. . . . Sh-sh," I said. *"Grils* approaching."

We lay down on our stomachs on the floor of the tree house and watched Tornid's two sister *grils* saunter to the Fabians' gate with Connie Ives, home from college for a few days. They stopped under Miss Alderman's tree, second only to Billy Maloon's in size, and they looked up at the drooping nest. Tornid and me watched them and we listened.

"Are you home for the summer?" C. *gril* Beatrice asked.

"Not yet," said Connie. "I will be on Decoration Day."

Can you beat that? I tell you. That's one reason I'm aiming to go there—to college. You get to go late in September, and you get to come home the end of May. Neat. Tornid and me listened for clues, like Black-Eyes saying, for instance, "We know what Timmy and Nicky do with all their spare time . . . they're . . ." And then she'd reveal the secret of the tunnel, if she knows it. But there were no clues. All the *grils* did was, they brought Connie up to date on Alley news, like about the white-bellied squirrel, the cross-eyed cat named King, and the visitor raccoon. Yechh! We had wanted to tell Connie about all those neat things.

Then the talk veered off onto sounds in the Alley houses. Me and Tornid pricked up our ears. Blue-Eyes said, "Sometimes in the nighttime I hear strange sounds, Connie, funny little noises. Mommy says they may be mice, or sparrows in the ivy talking in their sleep. . . . But I wish they wouldn't do it."

"Yez," said black-eyed *gril.* "And Mommy zayz maybe it'z juzt the oldnezz of the houzez . . . and they creak.

Zazha hearz the zoundz, too, and zee getz zcared and zee
crawlz into bed with Mommy and zhakez. Izzy and I, we
keep our door clozed and the door into the attic clozed zo
nothing can get out at uz. I zleep on the zide of the bed
that iz farthezt from the attic. That'z fair becauze Izzy iz
one year older. That iz fair, izn't it, Connie?"

"Zoundz fair," said Connie.

Yechh. Now she's got Connie, a girl in college, contaminated into using a "z" where an "s" belongs. Next thing
everybody'll be doing it—these things are catching.

Then LLIB came along. He'd heard part of the talk.
"And, yeah," he said. "But I know who really makes all
those sounds . . . it's a guy named Jimmy Mannikin . . . lives down below. . . . Sometimes you hear
him chipping on his work . . . banging pipes, banging
walls . . ."

We didn't hear the rest of LLIB's theories because everyone sauntered away. "Come on, Tornid," I said. "If LLIB
can hear us chipping, soon someone else will. No time to
lose."

We slid out of the tree house and hopped in the hidey
hole and located our word TRATS. No one had erased it or
added their two cents. Above, in the kitchen, Tornid's
mom was ironing. She had the television on. Her television
is in the living room in plain view from almost every spot
on the first floor, even from the kitchen. Tornid's mom
always has the television on, whether she's paying attention
or not. If someone comes to visit, she turns the sound off,
but she leaves the picture on not to miss the whole thing.
Sometimes you don't know whether she hears you or not.
You wonder if you are interrupting something special she
had in mind to watch. Then you realize this isn't so. She
just likes to have TV on all the time—it's her custom. Not

like in Jane's house where it's the custom to hide it and let it get dusty.

The sound was on now—no visitors within—and it came out to us via the dining-room windows. It was going on about the weather. We listened to what it was going to do. We've caught this habit from the grownups who always want to know what it's doing out. It said strong winds and rain were predicted for early in the day, continuing through nightfall, all up and down the Atlantic seaboard. Small-craft warnings already in effect from Cape Hatteras to Kennebunkport, Maine.

"We have to work fast, Torny, old boy, old boy," I said. "Ride the storm out in the tunnel, if possible . . ."

"Yeah," said Tornid.

Our hole, thanks to the help from, probably, the visiting raccoon, if not from smoogmen below, eager to get out, was very big now. We worked hard. Each of us wanted to be first to feel nothing . . . that is, tunnel air . . . to be in the tunnel at last. Suddenly the wall around TRATS crumbled. I yanked Tornid away. I poked my arms and my head into the wide hole. Loose stones and gravel slipped down to somewhere. We had made a breakthrough into somewhere! Probably the office marked T.N.F. on the map.

I wriggled back out, wiped my face, cleaned my glasses, looked at Tornid through the lower part of them, and said, "Tornid. We are, I believe we are, at this moment . . . mark the time on the chart . . . 9:45 . . . about to make our entrance into the tunnel, the office of it marked T.N.F. on the map."

"We are?" said Tornid. "Copin. Will this tunnel be our tunnel? Our own tunnel?"

"Cripes!" I said. "Tornid," I said. "This tunnel is a

tunnel for all the Alley, all. . . . Even though we are the discoverers of it and we were the ones who paid attention to the words of Hugsy Goode and we get into it first, see where it goes, still it is for all in the Alley. And for Grandby College, a tunnel to make it proud," I said. "Same as if you get to the moon first and plant a flag there, the moon will still be the moon for all the world."

"And universe," said Tornid.

"So now, Tornid, since this breakthrough happens to be under your house, you can be the first to feel into it. Reach your hands and arms in, your head, get in as far as you can, smell, feel around. I'll hang onto your legs so you won't slide in and disappear. Wiggle a leg when you want out."

He did this. Soon he wiggled a leg. I pulled him out. He said, "Can't feel bottom, can't feel a wall except the crumbly part of this one where we dug, can't feel anything, and it all smells like it's been smelling all along, like rubble."

"Must be the way tunnel air smells around here," I said. I stuck my head, shoulders, and arms in, and I felt nothing either. I said, "Tornid. We have penetrated the wall of the tunnel because all we feel is nothing . . . unless . . . this wall is part of your cellar. . . . Must check on that. Make a note of the time—10:00 A.M."

He wrote "10" in chalk on TRATS. He carries out orders well.

We went into the Fabians' house. We wanted to go down the cellar and make sure we hadn't dug the hole into it instead of the tunnel. Tornid's mom was still ironing, one eye on the board, the other on television. She can even type Frank Fabian's papers, one eye on them, the other on TV. It's a gift. I like her; I wish she liked me.

"And . . . where are you going?" she asked.

"Down cellar," said Tornid. "We're looking for something."

"OK," she said. "But come right back up. Remember, I saw a rat down there last week. Just now, I thought I heard him again."

We raced down the cellar steps. The windows that are over the washtubs are just as sooty inside as outside. Some of the vines planted by Hugsy Goode have even made it through the bricks and are beginning to spread over the inside, too. No one could possibly see through them to us chipping away outside. There wasn't any sign of the hole we had dug anywhere. So, *we had not dug into the Fabian cellar.*

It was a solemn moment. Solemnly we went back up and out, passing Tornid's mom and undaunted by her quizzical eyes. Yeah. Even with mind divided between TV and ironing, she can still look quizzical . . . at us. But she didn't ask any questions out loud.

We sat down on the bottom step of the Fabians' back stoop and ate some apples to strengthen us for the expedition. "Tornid," I said. "Now we know we are really on our way to somewhere." We felt blissful. What a life!

"Getting dark," said Tornid. "Daytime, but it's getting dark."

"You're right," I said.

I looked around. Wind, sudden wind, rustled the fresh green leaves of the Alley trees. A big plop of a raindrop suddenly fell on my head. Honest. It was so big, I thought it had made a hole in my scalp. "Look at my head," I said to Tornid. I bent over. "Do you see a hole there, a crater?"

"No-o. But I see a puddle," Tornid said.

"Cripes!" I said. "It's the rain they said was coming."

It came all right. Suddenly, like someone turning on a giant faucet, a giant rain came down. We ran for the tree house and sat cross-legged in the middle of it under the red and white striped canopy. In a minute you couldn't even see Tornid's back door, the rain was so dense.

"It's a squall," I yelled. Wind beat the hard rain into us, and we were soaked. Tornid tore into his house and got his boots and yellow slicker, and I into mine and did the same; and we beat our way against the rain and up the Alley to where the Circle used to be. Coming back down to where the drain was, we were swept along, scarcely able to stand up. "It's a flood!" I yelled. "The Alley River! Tell Mr. Lee!" I yelled.

Tornid couldn't even hear me. The Alley River couldn't all get down into the drain outside Billy Maloon's, and it couldn't all get into the other drains at the ends of the top part of the T of the Alley. Our boots were filled with water. We might drown, so we took them off. Huge ponds collected in the yards of the houses facing Larrabee Street, the low end of the Alley, and the biggest pond was outside Tornid's back stoop. The pond there was already up to the second step. One more step and it would race into the kitchen, through the house, and out the front door to Larrabee Street.

We waded through the pond of T.N.F. and took shelter in Tornid's vestibule. "Soon your house will be flooded and float away like a brick ark," I said to Tornid.

Tornid became frightened. He was nearly crying because now his house was like a ship and might float away. He's always worried about ships sinking ever since he saw a movie on TV about the sinking of the *Titanic.* He worries about whether his mom would leave his dad behind on the sinking ship and leap into the lifeboat for the sake of the children back home. So he said he had to go in now to rescue his dad, in case his mom had her hands full with LLIB and the rest.

"Cluck!" I bellowed. "There aren't any icebergs around, like with the *Titanic.* This is *rain,* not ocean."

We both went in anyway to catch our breaths and shake our wet hair all over Sasha, who got behind Tornid's mom. Both the moms were in there, scowling their heads off. At first I thought it was me. I suppose I get what's coming to me. "You reapeth what you soweth," a saying of Mr. John Ives.

But right now the moms' scowls were directed against the Commodore. Too bad he wasn't here to see and hear.

"Look at that lake outside the door! Look at those drains out there in the Alley! Why can't the Commodore fix the drains, once and for all, have more of them built if necessary and let the water run off instead of seeping down into our cellars? I wish he had ten children to wade through a lake like that into his immaculate house, have to put rubbers on them and take them off them for weeks after the rain stops . . . takes that long for the pond to dry up . . ."

"And break their necks when it freezes over in the winter . . ." chimed in my mom.

"Doesn't thaw out till spring . . ." said Tornid's mom.

"But you know what he says: 'Get the kids to stop stuffing things in the drain . . . they take the grate off and stuff everything in . . .' "

Tornid and me listened enthralled to this tirade of the moms, who are always worth listening to. Tornid's dad didn't even know it was raining out. He was baking a cake —he's good at that, and pies, especially lemon. So, everything being snug harbor inside, no dad needing rescue, Tornid and me went back out into the hard rain. Lots of Alley children were out now, and tiny ones took off their red sneakers and watched them race away. It was about as good as the blizzard last March.

Connie Ives came along. She'd thought it was hailing, the rain banged so on the windowpanes. She was barefoot, too, like us. Connie's hair is long and blond. But in a second it was as dark brown as shiny wet seaweed. She laughed and screamed. Connie enjoys things so much, you can't help but watch her. She licked the rain off her cheeks, and her eyelashes were stuck together and blacker than ever . . . looked like fake ones. It's lucky that girls get into that stage finally and outgrow Contamination.

We—Blue-Eyes, Black-Eyes, all Fabians, all Carrolls —careened into each other. I said to Tornid, "The rain washes off the Contamination, so you can breathe in the presence of *grils*."

The two stranger girls watched all this from their dining-room window. "Come on out!" yelled Blue-Eyes and

Black-Eyes. All the Fabians have a friendly streak. But the two stayed in.

Suddenly I remembered! "Tornid," I said. "We should have stopped up the hole we made down there into the tunnel. The river will pour down there. Yikes!"

"Yikes!" said Tornid.

Too late now. What would we see tomorrow when we lowered ourselves down? A river? An under-the-Alley river? Yikes!

Chapter 13

Midnight River on
Larrabee Street

River! I mean it! Call the rain river in the Alley a river? Listen to this if you want to hear about rivers! In the middle of the night I waked up. Steve waked up. The entire family including my mom and dad waked. What did we hear? It didn't sound like rain. It sounded like a waterfall —Niagara, Victoria—or like a vast river, the Mississippi —something gigantic whooshing and swooshing—like the roaring Rio Grande.

We got out of bed, raced downstairs, and looked out the front windows. There was a flood, a real river on Larrabee Street racing along a mile a minute. It didn't come into our street, Story Street, which slopes down into Larrabee. It tore down Larrabee toward Gregory as though it just had to make the green light there. Rushing to the upstairs back windows, we saw that the river made a left turn on Gregory and whooshed itself around the corner . . . because Larrabee begins to go uphill there.

It wasn't a temporary river that came and went like a lost river might do. It kept on coming and churning. My mom and dad got dressed. "Oh, dear," said my dad. "And I only just got to sleep . . ." Some grownups don't like something novel like a river on Larrabee Street. My mom had the baby in her arms. Holly spoke only in whispers to man and child alike because of the unusualness of the occasion. We all put on something and went out front and stood on the porch.

All the neighbors were coming out in strange garb, and some walked toward the wrought-iron gate of the fence that encircles the campus. Mrs. Stuart had curlers in her hair and didn't care and went to the gate, too.

Then Tornid's mom came to the Alley gate, saw us on our porch, and said, "Why don't you all come into our house? You'll have a better view. All the kids are up and looking out the front windows."

We did this. "It's a come-as-you-are party," said Tornid's mom. The moms and dads had some coffee, and the moms exchanged witty remarks about the way people outside were dressed—Mr. Stuart in his fishing boots, for instance. The moms were making a party out of the occasion. It was like New Year's Eve. But no one played the piano or sang "Auld Lang Syne" because they had to watch the river.

There wasn't any end to this river. It came and came and rose higher and higher and swooped over the sidewalk. It might come through the Fabians' front door and go out the back and join up with the ponds created by the rains. Then this little group of houses at the top of the Alley T would be marooned. Tornid stayed close to his dad, ready to save him, if necessary. This was something! We all had sodas. "Rot your teeth," said my mom, but she gave in, for just this once, there being no cider in the house or juice.

Now, there was Mr. Stuart in his fishing boots, joined by John Ives, who, unlike my dad, loves anything exciting. If there isn't any excitement going on, he makes some. He rants about something. He was barefoot and had his trousers rolled up like a clammer. They started to wade across the raging river. "John, come back, come back," yelled Jane Ives. And Connie said, "Dad*dee!*"

But they went anyway. And Connie and Jane Ives came into Tornid's house and joined all of us at the windows. Other neighbors came in, and if there had been food, a different dish brought by each different mom, it would have been like potluck days of olden times in the Alley. We saw John Ives and Mr. Malcolm Stuart make it across the river and be safe on the other side. They were joined by some students from the dormitory, and all disappeared up Larrabee Street to see where the river was coming from. After a while they came back, sopping wet and exhausted. They came in Tornid's house, and this is what they said.

John Ives said, "A water main broke up there at the corner of George and Larrabee. The houses on, and next to, the corners may crumble. God's blessing no car was coming along at the moment of the break. But cars parked near the corners were whooshed up into the air ten feet and landed upside down, on lawns—anywhere. Poor Mrs. Allessandro, my secretary . . . I helped evacuate her.

People are still being evacuated. Some had to be guided from rooftop to rooftop. The students helped me and Malcolm rescue fainting ladies and carry them to safety. A person on George Street had gotten a rowboat out of his cellar —why anyone has a rowboat in his cellar in Brooklyn beats me, but that's Brooklyn for you . . . full of surprises as well as churches . . ."

John Ives was happy and excited. He's a great storyteller. Sometimes he shouts. It comes down in his family, Jane Ives says, telling stories well, from generation to generation. His grandfather had the gift, his mother, and now Connie herself . . . that's three generations right there. "A magnificent sense of drama," says Jane Ives about them all. But not now . . . she isn't saying that now. Now, she is listening as we all are to the account of the flood.

Mr. Stuart said, "Sure was awful. Terrible. Roaring river." He never says very much.

John Ives was speaking again. "And don't let anyone say one thing against our students. They were right there, right on the spot, before police, firemen—anyone. *They* made trips into houses, *they* rescued children and the aged and carried them to a judge's house, an uncle of poor Mrs. Allessandro's, over near Myrtle. . . . I am very proud of them, our students, very proud," he said.

Mr. Stuart spoke. "Yes, indeed. Proud."

John Ives said, "I won't hear to anybody running down our students . . . those with beards and those without. Art students, architecture, food sciences . . ."

Mr. Stuart spoke. "Hm-m-m . . . didn't see any from science . . ."

Mr. John Ives said, "Oh, yes there were, Malc . . . you don't have to worry about your own students. They were there, too, along with all the other students, from all the schools, from all the dorms and houses around here, barefooted, pants and pajamas rolled up, rescuing people right and left, handing little ones and frail old ones out windows, carrying them on a man-made chain across the gushing water. They were heroic."

Mr. Stuart spoke. "Heroic."

Mr. John Ives said, "Where they got that rowboat . . . beats me. Ingenuity. That's what our students have. And I want you to know that I've worked on campuses all over the country . . . north, south, east, and west, even England . . . and I have never met a finer bunch of students than ours here at Grandby College. Dedicated. They rise to an occasion. . . . God's blessing . . . a miracle . . . that no one was driving down Larrabee. That would have been the end of him . . . whoo-oosh him up in the air. He'd—they'd—never have survived."

Mr. Stuart spoke again. "Never. Pretty bad . . . killed . . . sure. . . . Might have been. You never know."

Loud and clear John Ives said, "Yes, we can be proud of our students all right. Fine chaps. Who's responsible for an accident of this sort? Water! What a waste of good water! Think of the drought of the past two summers, and we might, in spite of the two inches yesterday, have another this summer . . . reservoirs still low. . . . How we have saved water . . . not bathed . . . not watered the grass (look at the grass on the campus!—burnt tan already and it's not even June). Drought! Yet they let this water come pouring out of a faulty main that they should have known about and fixed long ago. Now they can't even locate the break . . . where it is. Ts! And where's it all going, our good water? Roaring down Larrabee. Can't even get into the drains. Poor Mrs. Allessandro . . . she's my secretary . . . one of those who fainted. . . . She'll move, she'll move . . . and then where'll I be without a secretary?"

Sasha licked Mr. John Ives's feet.

But he went on in his peppery southern way. " 'Politics. Politics, politics, child. Politics.' That's what my mother always used to say when the price of cotton fell . . . 'It's politics, child. Politics.' "

We were getting sleepy. All the sodas gone, we drank water from the faucet to have some before it all rolled away, until my mom said maybe we should boil it first. But we were enthralled by Mr. John Ives. It was like being on the banks of the River Kwai, I thought.

John Ives said, "You'd think someone in the Water Department or Con Ed would have a map showing where the bungs are so they could turn them off. Efficiency? Never mind. Let's pray . . . pray that our fine new mayor will get things running right . . ."

I said to Tornid in a whisper, "They should draw a map or plan of the under-Brooklyn like we have of the Alley and then go and find the bungs. . . . If they don't know, they could at least guess . . ."

Mr. Malcolm Stuart said with gloom, "I dun-no-o."

While warming his feet on Sasha, Mr. Ives said, "At least our mayor is an honest mayor. He was even on the spot just now. I saw him. I was helping poor little Mrs. Allessandro out. Someone said the mayor was going to bung up the leak like the boy did in 'The Leak in the Dike.' Some sarcastic remark made by some wise guy, the sort that blames the mayor for everything including snow."

I like the mayor, too. I wondered if he had come across the river by helicopter. Perhaps he hadn't even read my letter yet with all these floods and fires and other terrible things to go to.

Mr. John Ives went to the window. "My golly!" he said. "There he is again, the mayor!"

"John Ives must have ESP, too," I whispered to Tornid.

Everyone crowded to the window and rapped and waved. In spite of the rushing noise of the water, the mayor heard us and he waved back. He had his pants rolled up like John Ives and might be barefooted, likewise. After that, everybody went home to their own houses and to bed because the water stayed at about the same level and wasn't coming through anyone's front door.

Next morning everybody felt like the day after New Year's Eve. Some took medicine. But the river had stopped. They got it stopped at 6:00 A.M., the radio said. There were some pictures in the *Times*. You could see John Ives and Mr. Malcolm Stuart with his fishing boots on. Also the mayor shaking hands with Father Hanley, the minister of the church at the corner of Gregory. He had a pot of coffee in his hand and some paper cups and was sitting on the seesaw in the park opposite Tornid's.

It was Saturday. Tornid and me looked at the mess left on Larrabee Street for a while. Pebbles, beer cans, sand, rubble, old tires, burnt tin cans from some incinerator! John Ives was out there again, this time trying to help clean up some of the mess. He can't stand messes like this and was muttering to himself. Even on non-mess days he stomps way across the campus to pick up some litter someone has littered. "Eyesore," he says. Once John Ives got out a newspaper all by himself named *The Grandby Growl*. In it he raged about things that are wrong on the campus, because the real college newspaper named *The Grandby Owl* does not rage hard enough for him. Now he's probably working up his rage enough to get out *The Grandby Growl* again . . . vol. 1, no. 2. I hope so.

I said, "Tornid, once we get down in the tunnel, we can

get out a newspaper in the office that may be under Jane Ives's house, name it *The Tunnel Trumpet.*"

"Or *The Underground Gazette,*" said Tornid.

"*¿Quién sabe?*" I said.

"*Sabe,*" he said. "We can write about the river in it," he said.

The river had been fun while it was going on. Too bad it couldn't stay always.

"But now, Torny, old boy, old boy," I said. "On with Operation Tunnel."

Chapter 14

Trats

So, back to the hidey hole! Well. Right now the hidey hole was one big mush hole, water seeping into it from the marsh the Fabians' yard had turned into. I said to Tornid, "If Hugsy Goode still lived here, he'd probably plant water lilies and put polliwogs in."

But the sun, just like it was saying on television, was out good and strong and ought to dry things out. We rolled up our pants like John Ives and the mayor and felt around in the hidey hole with our bare legs. Ooze, nothing but ooze, and the squash vines covered with mud. But in their waterproof sack our supplies were safe and dry. We'd put the big tools like shovels and picks back in our cellars. Now, in the sack, were our small and important things— flashlights, shillelaghs, rope, string, food (a couple of apples, some raisins, some chocolate . . . you can stay alive a long time on these), my water canteen Billy Maloon gave me when he went off to college—that's about it besides a few things we had in our pockets.

I heard the sound of gurgling water down below. Water from the big rain must have gotten down there. Might be a river or a canal down there now. And those were things I hadn't drawn in any of my plans.

"Listen, Tornid," I said. "You hear that? You hear that gurgling sound down below? Means there's a river, an underground lost river, lost in our tunnel that is under the

Alley, the tunnel of Hugsy Goode. You can hear it, wandering from one office to another, not knowing where to end up at. The lost river of the alley under the Alley."

"Yikes!" said Tornid.

"Yes," I said. "Like all rivers, it has to rise somewhere, and this one has risen in your backyard, in the rain pond there. And it has to flow somewhere, and it has decided to flow through the tunnel under the Alley. And where does it flow to? Where is its emptying-out place? If you have picked up any geography . . . I have in spite of the crummy social studies book, Grade Six . . . you know that a river has to begin and has to end—empty into something bigger than it, its mouth—maybe a sea or an ocean. Where is this Alley tunnel river's mouth?"

"I dun-*no*-o," said Tornid.

"I'll tell you," I said. "Doesn't have one. Has a beginning, here in the hidey hole, spilling over from that rain pond of yours—we'll name it Lake Fabian. But it has no ending, mouth, or there would be a big lake or something in the neighborhood. That's what makes this river gurgling down there a 'lost' river, just like all the other lost rivers in the world. They don't get to go anywhere, just get themselves lost, winding around underground, this one winding from one tunnel place to another—consult the map. You should be glad this lost river decided to begin in the section of the map marked T.N.F."

Tornid said, "We should have a boat for when we get down there. Wonder what that student did with that rescue boat last night?"

"I'll find out," I said. "I'll ask John Ives. And you're right. We don't know how deep the water is. It may be more like canals down there. Then we'd need gondolas— it may be like an underground Venice."

"It's spooky," said Tornid. "I wish it wasn't there. Before, there was just plain tunnel. Now there's a river lost, or canals . . ."

"Just makes the excavations even more exciting," I said. "We may have to redraw our plans after we've been down."

"I just wish water hadn't come into it," said Tornid. "I liked the old plans better. Once I went in a boat in the Funny House somewhere and it was dark. And we went into a tunnel. And we came upon skeletons, and I thought they were real. And sometimes the top of the tunnel was so low you had to scrouch down. And I was scared. And sometimes you'd go around another bend and a monster or a big snake would raise its neck and scream and hiss at you. And I was scay-ared."

"You won't be scared in our own tunnel, or of our river, Torny, old boy," I said. "Only just a little bit."

"I dunno," said Tornid. "Get me out of here was what I thought in that other tunnel I was in that had water in it, the only other tunnel I ever been in. So far. And I hope I won't be that scared in ours."

"It's more fun if you don't feel too safe," I said. "They, smoogmen, may be down there, or . . . may not be."

"*¿Quién sabe?*" said Tornid.

The sun was getting around to our side where it might help dry out the hidey hole. So we went up in the tree house to wait for the water to seep away. I had some wads of string in my pocket. "Here," I said. "Wind. We'll need string and thread so we can find our way back to TRATS if we go by foot and not by raft or boat. We'll need lots of string. You might go over to Mrs. Harrington's. She likes you . . . never mind if she kisses you—forget it . . . and she has lots of string. She may give you a bunch of it she's picked up and saved through the years. It's why she's so rich, saves this string, and she'd probably like to have it untangled and wound up, and maybe she'd go fifty-fifty with you. She is a hundred and one."

But Tornid didn't want to go.

"You'll never get ahead," I said. But anyway, just then, there was a commotion outside the Alley gate. The moms were about to set off in our little blue bus. "We're going to Job Lots," my mom shouted.

"Don't go away," said Tornid's mom. And she and all the *grils* piled in along with my mom.

Well, that was fair. It was the *grils'* turn. It's not me and Tornid's turn. We stayed in the tree house, waiting for them to go. Then there they went, jabber-jabber, in my mom's little blue bus that we went all the way to Mexico in, lived there for one year, learned *¿Habla usted?* and

much more, and came back in. There were five of us kids
that went. We came back with one more, Branch, making
six, so's we outnumber the Fabians—they only have five.

We didn't wave to them—the Job Lots expeditioners.
We turned our backs, looked sullen, spat—I did anyway
—as they drove off so they'd see we felt left out and be
sorry. But the minute they were out of sight on Larrabee,
we slid down the slide, got rid of a bunch of little guys ooz-
ing in Lake Fabian (they were from up the Alley)—told
them to go dig in the Nagels' yard . . . there was gold
there—and we flopped down on a sort of dried-out space
beside the hidey hole. We listened and we heard it again,
the sound of gurgling water, our lost river again, as lost
as ever.

But we didn't care. "True explorers take what comes,"
I said.

"Come what, come may," Tornid said.

So we rolled up our pants and stepped into the hidey
hole. Squ-ish! You'd of thought we were on a clamming
beach off the state of Connecticut. Our hole was bigger
than ever now, thanks to the rain. Rain and raccoon, our
two allies so far in the Alley.

I have a large foot. My family all have big feet. My
mom says it's the wheat germ she sprinkles on cereal and
just about everything else she gets a chance to. Not bad.
So I stuck one of my big feet into the hole we'd made and,
just like the day before the rain, all I felt was nothing.

"Time to get busy," I said. "Before they get back from
Job Lots." We got all our things—shillelaghs, flashlights,
rope, string, food—out of the sack and prepared for the
descent into the tunnel.

This might be *the* day.

We tied one end of my strong rope around Hugsy
Goode's peach tree—that he planted from a peach pit—

and made sure it was firm. We hopped in the hidey hole and shoved the other end of the rope, knotted to make it heavy, down into the hole. No splash. I pulled it back up. It wasn't wet. Maybe the tunnel river had already gotten itself altogether lost. *¿Quién sabe?* I would soon.

We put our sneakers in the waterproof sack to leave them behind and be dry as possible when we returned—if we did. Tornid has a small regular sort of flashlight. But mine is a big red one my mom bought me once at Job Lots during a friendly period. I clamped it on my belt around my waist so my hands and arms would not have too much to carry. I slung my canteen over my shoulder. I have learned to drink out of the canteen with it slung over my left shoulder, the way I've seen them do in some villages in Mexico, also in movies, and to spit the water out and wipe my mouth with the back of my hand.

"Agua," I said. "Means water. Remember that, in case it comes up on an S.A.T. some day."

"There's so much to learn," said Tornid.

"You'll get the hang of it all," I said. "Steve did."

I was going down first. I tied the knotted end of the rope around my waist below the flashlight and let out a couple of feet of rope. I held onto the rope with both hands. "Tornid," I said. "When I jerk the rope, let out some more. And hand me down my shovel, shillelagh, or anything else I ask for. Don't drop anything on my head . . ."

"Yeah. No," said Tornid.

"Here I go, then. If I never come back, dial 911 . . . that's the police. Or call my dad."

"Good-by," said Tornid.

And down I went into the unknown from location TRATS.

Chapter 15

The Tunnel of Hugsy Goode—
Descent No. 1

As I lowered myself down the rope, I took in a deep breath of upper Brooklyn smog air, not knowing what to expect below, river . . . what. . . . Tornid and me often practice holding our breaths. I can hold mine for one minute without busting open my lungs. It pays to practice all things. Holding breath to get past *grils,* practicing being blind in the Alley, counting the number of steps from the drain to where the Circle used to be, and to other points —all would come in handy in the darkness beneath me. We were experts in groping and holding breaths.

I clung to the edge of the hole. Stomach to wall, I eased myself down. I let myself down some more. All Tornid could see of me now were my arms, neck, and head.

Tornid laughed. "You look like a puppet," he said.

I blew my breath out and up at him. "Cut that out, cluck," I said. "Want to make me laugh and da-rown laughing?"

"No," he said.

I stayed where I was a minute and felt around with my feet. I swung my left foot around first. I felt nothing behind me. But far to the left, I felt solid wall. I thought it must be the wall separating the tunnel from the cellar. I swung my right foot around. Behind me, it also felt nothing; but to my right my toes felt more of the wall I was leaning against. Must be a wall of the tunnel, I thought.

100

I signaled to Tornid to let out some more rope. He did. I lowered myself some more. I am a human fly, I thought.

I looked back up. There was Tornid. His face looked large from this eerie angle, halfway down into a—I hope —*the* tunnel. "Can you see me?" I said.

"Yeah," he said. "You sound funny."

"It's still me," I said.

From now on my life depended on Tornid. I knew he would not let me down. Or, rather, he *would* let me down. That's what he was supposed to do. A pun. Get it?

I tugged three tugs. He let down some more rope. I kept going down. I had a feeling I was near the bottom and would soon touch. It's my ESP. "Pass me down my shillelagh," I said. I needed it to measure the river with, if there was one. Holding onto the rope with my right hand, pressing my stomach against the crumbly wall to balance myself, I grabbed my shillelagh and it was like a sword.

Tornid looked in. "Hurry up," he said. "Is there a tunnel or isn't there a tunnel? I want to come down, too."

"I am hurrying, cluck," I said. "Do you think it's easy finding tunnels, lost river, or whatever it is I'm finding? Crud."

"Are *they* there?" he asked.

"Who?" I asked, turning my head around suddenly to take *them*—"who"—by surprise.

"I don't know," said Tornid. "Smoogmen . . ."

"Shut up, ya dumb cluck!" I said. "You want them to hear us?"

The sound of Tornid's voice gave me courage. I knew he would get help come what, come may. So, waving my shillelagh, saying *"Hasta la vista,"* I let go of the rope and dropped. I just decided to drop, that's all.

I landed on solid pavement, not in a river, not even a stream. I took in my first gulp of tunnel air. It tasted like a long-locked-up cellar. I turned my flashlight around so it would shine into wherever I was. I waved my shillelagh to scatter and terrify all beings, visible and nonvisible . . . smoogmen or whatever. . . . I said, *"¿Cómo está usted y ustedes?"* because a great deal of Spanish is spoken around here, and if the smoogmen were Spanish, they would know I was a friend.

My eyes grew accustomed to where I was. By cracky! I was at the beginning of some sort of narrow passageway. It was tall enough to stand up in, not one of the crawl-through sort such as some I had put in the plans.

"Come on down," I yelled up at Tornid. I needed my pal. I thought I saw eyes up ahead and needed Tornid's good eyes to say yes he saw them or no he didn't. Could be an hallucination . . . a tunnel mirage. "Shinny down the rope," I said. "I've untied it from me."

Tornid's skinny bare legs came into sight, then the rest of him. I reached up to help him down, and he was the second boy to set foot in what we suppose is alley tunnel and to leave footprints here, muddy ones from the hidey hole of Hugsy Goode.

"Is *this* the tunnel?" Tornid asked. "It doesn't look like the tunnel in the Funny House where I went that time."

"That's because it's an alley tunnel, cluck!" I said.

"What am I stepping on?" asked Tornid. "It's hard and cold. But it doesn't wiggle."

We flashed our lights down. It wasn't anything alive, or even dead like a fossil. It was a key, a huge and rusty antique key, always a good omen when you are on a quest. I picked it up . . . I save keys, like Mrs. Harrington saves string . . . and I put it in my gunny sack, the first important find in the alley tunnel.

We took a few steps, and swoosh! Suddenly we found we were walking in water. But, relax. Not a great, sworling,

swirling river, just a small, not deep—I tested it with my
shillelagh, and it was two inches here—inky black, gurgling stream. That's what we'd heard up top. Probably,
just like we'd thought, the great rain had rushed in down
here through the hole me and Tornid had dug. Probably,
usually rain doesn't get down here, and when we got out,
we'd close up our hole tight so no more could come in.
No hope for an underworld Venice with gondolas going
from tunnel office to tunnel office, which we could have
had if there had been a river. Too bad. No Grand Canal.

"OK, Tornid," I said. "Here we are now." I showed him
where on the map. "Here, in what I suppose is an arm of
the main tunnel." I flashed my big light way ahead.

"It's just like you drew it," said Tornid. He was not
surprised.

"Yes," I said. "So here we are, alone here in the alley
tunnel, the part marked T.N.F."

"Not much of an office," said Tornid.

"The office may be built way inside the wall. First we explore the tunnel itself, then we find the offices . . . you and me alone, without any C. *grils* to bother us." On the wall I wrote T.N.F.

"Named after me," said Tornid proudly. "But if we're alone, whose eyes are those then?"

So there were eyes up there, then. We stood stock-still and did not speak. Were those the eyes of *them,* whoever they are, smoogmen, or what? Anyway, the eyes were not tunnel mirage, because it is rare for two different boys to have the same mirage, I read somewhere. This one set of eyes might be a lookout guy, and others might be everywhere, eying us—just two boys from on top—with deadly precision as we stood like stone in the area marked T.N.F.

At last, *"Buenos días,"* I said out loud to break the spell and in Spanish in case it were the Spanish smoogman. *"Amigos,"* I said.

"Bless Maud!" said Tornid in a squeaky voice. That is a saying of his gram's. He whispered to me, "They won't know who Maud is. They'll think she is your mother and be scay-ared and run away."

What should we do? Climb back up, or be brave and go on and chase the eyes' owner away? "Well, Tornid," I said. "There are always eyes in a tunnel. Now, there's just one set of eyes that we can be sure of, and they haven't winked or budged. I have my flashlight turned on them. If they come nearer, I wave my shillelagh, we say the powerful words that make the beams of my light fatal, we say scram and also TEAB TI (that's beat it, backwards, remember), and see what happens."

Brandishing our shillelaghs, we advanced on the eyes. "Let's hope whoever or whatever those eyes belong to doesn't back off, and us not know where it's backed off to, where it might turn up next and perhaps . . ."

"Bite . . ." said Tornid.

"Right," I said. "Grab us!"

"Shoo!" said Tornid. But it didn't shoo.

We proceeded very slowly toward the eyes, and the eyes' owner just stayed right there. Then, at the same identical moment, Tornid and me guessed, and we said together . . . "Raccoon!" We could have made a wish but saved it for some other time when there was less to do.

Yes. Those eyes were the eyes of the visiting raccoon. Now we could see his stripes . . . and there couldn't be a whole tribe of raccoons living around our Alley, so he must be the one who'd looked in the window at us, he just must like the neighborhood and was exploring, an exploring raccoon, like we are exploring boys.

Here he was! We hadn't seen him for days. Last we knew of him he had helped dig our hole in the hidey hole. Perhaps he had slipped in and couldn't get back out. Or maybe he just decided to go exploring. That's the way with raccoons . . . curious. So here he was, now, down in our tunnel.

We stepped back to TRATS in case he wanted help in getting out. And we said, "Here, raccoon. Here." But he didn't come. He gave us the same unblinking stare, just as curious about us now as he had been on the night of first acquaintance through the Fabians' window. We stared back at him. None of us stirred.

Then, suddenly, with a flash of his pretty bushy tail, the raccoon leaped, but not onto our shoulders to get up and out of the tunnel. He leaped way ahead of us and disappeared from sight.

"He must have turned a corner!" I said. "He's showing

us the way. Man, oh man!" I said. "There really is more tunnel than just this small corridor!"

"Sure," said Tornid. "You drew more."

A key and a raccoon. Two things so far. "Tornid," I said. "That raccoon seems to like it down here. A tunnel is an unusual place for a raccoon."

"Yeah," said Tornid. "But maybe he thought the river he heard gurgling down here, like we did, maybe he thought it was a river lost from the country, like him, and that it would lead him back to his old home . . ."

"I tell you what, Tornid. That raccoon is a sport raccoon. Not a sport, like an athlete or a good guy, but a sport meaning a creature or a person that behaves in a different way from others of its sort."

"A sport raccoon," said Tornid.

I felt great. What with my pal, Tornid, being with me on the expedition, and with an unhurt, alive, and well raccoon guide, who knows what we would find next? We were not in the Fabian cellar. We were not in some fancy sewer like they have in Paris that you can read about in the book of Jean Valjean—Steve told me the highlights. We were right here in the tunnel I deduced the existence of, thanks to the ESP of Hugsy Goode.

"Yes, boy," I said to Tornid. "We are in a passage under your walk to your back door. Soon we should be in the main six feet high, three feet wide tunnel of the under alley . . . I think . . ."

"Yippee!" said Tornid. "When we turn the corner . . . then we will know."

"Yes," I said triumphantly. "And Torny, old boy, old boy. I will mark it here. With this chalk I will name this tunnel the *Tunnel of Hugsy Goode*."

I so wrote it on the wall with a neat piece of psychedelic

chalk my mom had brought home from some weird grown-up party. Tornid has a piece, too.

We made fitting signs over the words with our shille-laghs, meaning it was permanent and so labeled for all pos-terity.

Then we took our bearings.

Chapter 16

Into the Glooming

"Let's see," I said, studying our map by flashlight, holding it low so Tornid could see, too. "We're here, now, in area T.N.F. We're not going to explore around here right now to see where the T.N.F. office for "their" business might be. We're going to push right on and find out how long this passageway is . . . up top it's twenty feet to your gate from your back stoop. Down here, it should be at least twenty-five. Then there should be a bend into the main six feet high, three feet wide tunnel, the top part of the under-alley T. The raccoon disappearing like that means there must be a bend, or . . ."

"He might be in one of those wall bunk bed places we draw . . ."

"Might," I said. "And that's what we have to find out."

The things we had to find out! Like whether or not there's a circle at the end, still intact, not carted away. Maybe it was a gathering place for the people, human or smoogman, to hold meetings in, their children to play games in and turn their bikes around in . . . ¿quién sabe?

So now, business. A pale light from the hidey hole flecked the wall opposite us. And ahead, our flashlights broke the darkness with an eerie beam. We felt scared to go on into the glooming. We felt safe in this section named T.N.F.

"Where's the river?" asked Tornid. "I really was scared there'd be a river . . ."

"Well, it's gone and gotten itself lost, left just this trickle behind as a clue to tell where it's lost itself to," I said.

"Good riddance," said Tornid. "I'd be scared of a lost river down here."

"Well, it's gone. So now to get ready for us to go, too . . . raccoon and river both gone."

I tied the end of a ball of string to the knotted end of the rope we'd left dangling from the hidey hole. If anyone up top came along and tried to pull our rope up, the string would signal me. It was my telegraph system. Me and Tornid didn't want to be trapped down here, not until we fixed it up for us to camp in when we found out all about it. And there's no sense exploring a new tunnel or a maze without string to follow to get you back.

We wanted to tie Tornid's string to something different. We flashed our lights around T.N.F. By cricky! There was the other end of the big round pipe that's in the Fabians' yard on top. It jutted out to the left of our rope, had a hinged lid that was clamped on tightly. We tied Tornid's string around that.

"They must have used this big pipe as a vent," I said. "Tunnel vent . . ."

"Marked T.V. on top," said Tornid. "Maybe they used it to get people in and out of?" he asked.

"Not big enough for that," I said. "Not for some people, anyway."

"I know. Our moms," said Tornid.

So far, all I knew about this pipe was that it wasn't any pipe dream. It's real like everything else so far in this book. No elves, no little folk, fairies and such. There may be real smoogmen—don't know yet. But we are wide awake, we are not dreaming. This *is* real. We are in a tunnel under the

Alley. Why there *is* a tunnel may bug some people. Not me. Just *being* is reason enough for me. But we have to find it all.

So, now, here we are, strings tied, return route assured. Lost river really lost, raccoon not in sight, and us—Tornid and me—on our way into the glooming.

It was a spooky thing to do. We checked everything. We had our flashlights turned on—mine was still attached to my belt around my waist. We had our sacks strapped to our backs. We had our balls of string in one hand, our shillelaghs in the other held high like swords. We were going to use them, not only to fend off *them,* but also as divining rods to locate hollow places in the wall where secret offices might be. We gave one last look back at the pale light from the hidey hole . . . no one had closed the entranceway so far so we were still connected with human beings—life—and cautiously we stepped down the narrow passageway into the glooming.

Thusly we went.

At least a raccoon was down here with us. Here's hoping he wouldn't appear suddenly from somewhere— startle us. But, raccoons are friendly . . . just curious, that's all . . . I think . . .

"Tornid," I said. "Sport raccoon or not, it is unnatural for that fellow to stow himself away down here in a tunnel, trees being the natural habitat for raccoons. First he spies on us through your window . . . then he comes down here. Maybe he reports to *them* . . ."

"Oo-ooh, yeah," said Tornid. "A smoogman in disguise, *fur* disguise. Hey . . . but raccoons do like darkness, probably even sport ones do. Here, it's always darkness. This raccoon doesn't have to wait the way most raccoons do for the sun to set to have it dark, pitch-black darkness all the time."

"I hope you're right," I said.

"*¿Quién sabe?*" said Tornid. He's getting to speak Spanish very well.

We went on slowly, not to trip or fall in a pit. After about twenty-five steps . . . I made a note in my notebook . . . we came to the end of this ell of the tunnel. We knew it was the end—our flashlights showed just wall up ahead. But, would it turn a corner and continue?

It did. It made a sharp, squared-off turn left. On our right was nothing but wall. We flashed our light down this new corridor. We couldn't see the end of it. But we did see that it was a main three feet wide, six feet high tunnel as described in Chapter 1. It is almost beyond belief that everything is working out exactly as drawn in my guessed-at plan. I really should be an architect when I grow up, or a plumber. Maybe those little men in bunk beds will turn out to be real, too. Also, passageways you have to crawl through like the one to my PIT on the map.

Well, if we had felt scared to leave the pale slant of light from the hidey hole behind—our connection with Alley on top—imagine how we felt turning this corner! But we did it. We unwound some string, wrote "entrance to T.N.F." in psychedelic chalk on the wall outside the little corridor, and cautiously went on. No sign of the raccoon, be he friend or enemy in fur disguise, nothing . . . no eyes. Lost river still a mere trickle, winding up its affairs. No sign of any bones. Why think of bones, though, in a tunnel created, as far as we can see now, by man as part of the Alley and its twenty-seven houses?

There must be some reason for keeping the tunnel a secret, and bones may be the reason.

Tough on Hugsy Goode! Poor Hugsy had to move away before he could follow up his hunch. If he ever comes back to visit (he's a boy with a beard now, in college now, and

gets back and forth to it with a sleeping bag on his back
. . . neat!), will he ever be pleased to see his name in
psychedelic chalk written on a tunnel wall! It's not everyone gets to have a tunnel named after him. Hugsy's dream
come true.

But you can't say Hugsy put the idea of bones in our
heads. *The Brooklyn Eagle* gets the credit for that idea.
It told about those children that found those forty skeletons
in the rubble of those ancient homes they tore down in
Brooklyn Heights before they got around to proclaiming
that part of the city a landmark—a landmark like we hope
this tunnel will be, and the Alley and the Myrtle Avenue
El will be. Haven't heard from the mayor *yet!* What's the
matter with him, I wonder.

"Tornid," I said. "If we find bones, let's not act surprised. Let's not say, 'Yikes,' let's not run."

"Let's just say, 'Hurray!' " said Tornid.

We started down the alley under the Alley slowly, cautiously. Quiet? Wow! Sometimes we felt a vibration.

"Not an earthquake," I whispered.

"No," Tornid whispered.

"Trucks above tearing down Larrabee," I whispered.

"Yes," he whispered.

It was spooky down here, and we were whispering like
Holly in the presence of grownups.

"Hey," I whispered. "Why are we whispering? From
now on, when I have to whisper something, I'm going to
say it, not whisper it."

"Me, too," whispered Tornid, not wanting to be the first
to hear his voice.

My flashlight cast a long bright beam into the glooming. We were in the neat six feet high, three feet wide tunnel under what on top is the top of the T of the Alley. After
seventy-eight steps, as it is above anyway, we should be un-

der the Alley in back of Billy Maloon's house where there is the drain the kids stuff their things into. There, there must be another bend going up the long end of the T of the Alley. From it, we hoped to find an ell leading under Jane Ives's house and to her pit or office, the main one for business, as I had drawn it. I still hoped for a crawling, narrow type of passage there. But everything doesn't have to be exactly as I had drawn it. There are bound to be some surprises . . .

Suddenly Tornid whispered, "What's that?"

"What's what?" I asked, still whispering, too.

"That," whispered Tornid. "That, up there, straight ahead?"

Tornid has better eyesight than me, doesn't have to wear glasses, not even for reading. So he spots things faster. "Looks like a chair," he said.

I spotted it, too. " 'Tis a chair!" I said.

There, where we figured must be under Billy Maloon's back fence, there was a chair, facing itself up the vertical line of the T, if the tunnel alley was a T-shaped one, like the Alley above.

We stood still.

The chair was vacant, as far as we could tell, nothing visible anyway. But it looked as though it expected a sitter. We kept our lights on it and studied it. In all my plans, I had never drawn a chair, a human chair.

"Who do you think it's waiting for?" I asked Tornid, still whispering.

"I dun-*no*," whispered Tornid.

We took one more step forward. Nothing happened. Cautiously, step by step, we made our way to the chair.

"Maybe it's waiting for us?" said Tornid.

"You mean . . . some sort of trap?" I asked.

"Maybe . . ." said Tornid.

Chapter 17

Don't Sit in That Chair!

Tornid and me were puzzled. Here we'd been thinking about lost rivers, mazes, the Minotaur, bones and skeletons. Instead here was a human chair. It was a straight-backed chair with wooden arms and legs and rungs, and it had some kind of needlework on its faded red velvet seat. It faced up the under alley just the way Billy Maloon's house above did. It looked like a throne, vacant, waiting for a king.

It also looked kind of like the chair in Connie Ives's house named the Uncle Ham chair. Lots of chairs in Connie Ives's house have names. You can sit in some of the named chairs, the Uncle Ham chair for one, the Lincoln rocker for another. But not the George Washington chair. "Don't sit in that chair (the George Washington chair)," is one of the few don'ts of the Ives's house.

Since this chair in the tunnel looked like the Uncle Ham chair at the Ives's, one of the sitting-allowed chairs, we decided to sit in it, come what, come may. Tornid sat first. This was fair since he saw it first. No one said, "Don't sit in that chair."

I sat next.

The chair bugged me. It was the only piece of furniture down here, so far anyway. Usually there's no furniture in a tunnel that I ever heard of. I had sat down carefully, not to break it. Some dust blew out, but the chair didn't wobble. It was in good shape, just as good shape as the

Uncle Ham chair in the home of Connie Ives, where some dust blows out, too.

I crossed my legs. I asked Tornid, "What shall we name this chair? It looks like the Uncle Ham chair. Should we name it the Uncle Ham, Junior, chair? There's a man by that name in the family of Connie Ives as well as a just plain Uncle Ham."

We were speaking out loud now, not whispering, because a chair makes you feel you are in a parlor, not a tunnel. "I dun-*no* . . ." said Tornid. "I'll think."

I began to feel more and more at home, having this real chair to sit in that no one said not to sit in. If I had been a grown man and had a cigar, I would have smoked it. But, I reminded myself, it's not a good idea to feel too safe. I might be sitting on some invisible person, some smoogman, dust smoogman, maybe. "Keep on guard" is my motto in Alley above and alley below.

I shone my flashlight to my right. The beams reached the end, the wall at the end of the T.N.F. passageway. I shone it to my left. The beams reached the end there, too, another wall outside the Bernadettes' house above, the other end of the top of the T. Then I cast my beams far ahead, and they did not reach any end where we hoped a Circle might be. Too bad we couldn't string little electric lights up and down so we could see the whole of the under-alley T at once.

So far, except for the unexpected pleasure of a chair to sit on, all was according to my maps and plans. I felt for my map. There might be a pickpocket smoogman who'd already gotten a hold of it. But it was safe, and I drew a small square on it meaning chair, where the chair was.

"Copin," Tornid said. "This chair looks like a chair I saw in Maine once. They said, in that family where it was, that it was a beadle's chair."

"That's what we'll name it, then," I said. "The Beatles' chair."

"I said 'beadle,' not 'Beatle,' " said Tornid.

"Well, 'Beatle' is more up to date," I said. "And, so far, there hasn't been a chair named for them, not even in Jane Ives's house, where they name chairs and like the Beatles." I began to whistle softly "A long day's night," the chair made me feel that much at home in the tunnel.

"Long day's night," said Tornid. "That's what it is down here all right. Good place for raccoons," he said.

"And us," I said, feeling more and more nonchalant.

Tornid was standing beside me. I was sitting. His arm was on the arm of the chair. I felt like a king. The chair felt like my throne. "An artist should paint us here," I said. We stayed in this pose for a while, but there weren't any artists around to paint us, and no one with a camera either. Then an idea came to me.

"I think we should name this chair the *Throne of Hugsy Goode,*" I said, "not the Beatles' chair. All this alley tunnel, all we find in it is because of the ESP of Hugsy Goode."

So I wrote that name above the chair in psychedelic chalk.

"Can I write something somewhere on the wall with my chalk?" asked Tornid.

"Oh, sure," I said.

I poked around in front of the chair with my shillelagh. It hit something metal. It was a drain. "Hah!" I said. "That architect that planned this tunnel, he allowed for everything. That's where the lost river lost itself. The tunnel builder allowed for seepage."

"Ah," said Tornid.

I flashed my light straight up. There was a gurgling sound up there—from the drain, of course, outside the gate of Billy Maloon. Naturally the Alley drain couldn't be seen, and the sky couldn't be seen, or the tunnel would have been discovered long ago. The drain on top had to drain off to somewhere else . . . to the pipes under Larrabee, not to down here . . . or the alley tunnel could not have been kept secret all these years.

"Ah, yes," I said. "But time now, Tornid, old boy, old boy, to continue with the questing . . ."

"Can I sit a minute again before we go?" Tornid asked. "In the Throne of King Hugsy the Goode, now that it's named?"

"Sure," I said.

Tornid sat down. Then . . . I'm not kidding—it's enough to make the gooseflesh rise even now . . . we heard the words, DON'T SIT IN THAT CHAIR!

Tornid leaped up. We both leaped down the alley into the glooming toward T.N.F., home base. My flashlight was askew, and it cast beams anywhere except straight ahead.

We knocked into the wall at the end of the main tunnel and got bruised. We were glad we knew to turn right into the narrow passageway of T.N.F. to get back to our entrance into the hidey hole. There was the pale light from the world above slanting on the wall opposite our hole. What a relief! Escape was possible.

Our strings and threads were all tangled around our arms and legs, but somehow we got out. Tornid climbed on my shoulders and hoisted himself the rest of the way up the heavy rope. I then hoisted myself up the rope, muttering charm words ". . . taeb ti, taeb ti . . ." to keep things behind me from grabbing me and sucking me back, whoever or whatever those things might be that said those creepy words, DON'T SIT IN THAT CHAIR!

Tornid was shaking as badly as the day of the expedition to Myrtle Avenue when his dad took him by the hand and said not one word. I was shaking, too. We climbed up into the tree house to let our shakes subside. Nothing seemed to have followed us out, so after a while we began to shake less.

"Who could have said those words, DON'T SIT IN THAT CHAIR?" I asked.

"I dunno . . ." said Tornid. "The raccoon, maybe?" He gave his crackly little laugh that meant the remark could be taken as a joke or for real, however it struck me.

I said, "I've heard of a talking dog. But I never heard of a talking raccoon."

"He's a sport raccoon, though," said Tornid.

I said, "Yeah. But I don't think it was Racky."

"No, he wouldn't know how to speak English anyway," said Tornid. "If he did speak, he'd probably speak Raccoonese."

"How do you say, 'Don't sit in that chair!' in Raccoonese?" I asked.

Well, we began to laugh. After terror, and you find yourself safe, still alive and not hurt—intact, in fact—you have to have a laughing jag. We began to untangle our string and wind up the threads. We thought the whole thing over. Then we grew shivery again. We had not thought up the words. They were not on our map. They were real. Yikes!

Would we have the courage to go back down in the Tunnel of Hugsy Goode again?

Chapter 18

Courage, Mon Ami

French words, those are—*Courage, mon ami.* I don't know much French, just *ooh la la, oui,* and *au revoir.* Also this expression, *"Courage, mon ami,"* which I learned from my Contamination sister Star, who is taking up the language. And, brother! When I say "taking it up," I mean taking it up, and it is *ooh la la* every second. Oh yes, and also *Fermez la bouche,* which means in plain English, "Shut up!"

So now, Contamination Star not being around to correct the pronunciation (*courage* rhymes, in French, with garage), I spoke these French words to Tornid, and I translated them for him. "They mean," I said, "Courage, my friend."

These rallying words made Tornid laugh. He even slid down the slide from the tree house, walked to the hidey hole and back, to show how effective they were. Then he climbed back up for more *courage.*

I replenished the supply. *"Courage, mon ami,"* I said. I know I sounded exactly French because I sounded like Star. We laughed and we laughed, still reacting to our terror at the words we'd heard a few minutes ago in the underground town—if it had a chair in it, it must be some sort of town.

Two of the *grils*—they were the two stranger ones— were playing jump rope outside Billy Maloon's gate where the water drain is. The names of these two stranger *grils* are Marlene and Charlene. I have watched them from the Arps' tree. They don't count in Alley life yet—as far as Tornid and me go, anyway. We don't see them, they don't see us. They are agreeable about doing most of the turning when other *grils* jump rope with them. They have deadpan faces, chew gum, look blank, try not to make a false move. They sound like all *grils* saying jump-rope chants—I've heard they've brought some new ones to the Alley. I haven't heard these yet. Me and Tornid are too busy with our plans.

We fell into a reverie while untangling and rewinding our string and thread, which were an awful mess. Tornid did not like doing this. I told him that if an old lady like Mrs. Harrington of the age of one hundred and one could wind string and amass a fortune, so could we. "Wind!" I said. I did the untangling, he did the winding. "Wind!" I said, when I had a few inches. And he wound.

Then my mom and Tornid's mom drove up in the blue bus named Chiquita, and they and all the kids spilled out. They gathered at the Alley gate, which was locked. They all had "I accuse you" expressions on their faces. They stood there, at the gate, sighting the sight of Tornid and me sitting in the tree house, winding string.

My mom said, "Where have you been?"

My mom's voice can rend the air as loudly as her whistle or a blast on her cow horn.

I returned blast for blast. "Here!" I blasted.

"You have not!" she blasted. "We were here a little while ago and you were not here. No one had seen you . . . no one. You have been out of the Alley . . ."

"We have not!" I blasted. I put on the surly look expected of me, happy to comply.

But I was indignant and full of righteous feelings. Tornid and me had not been out of the Alley, *under* it,

yes, but not out of it, not over to Myrtle Avenue again. You could tell that is what they had supposed, not seeing me or Tornid anywhere around, seeing just the two stranger *grils* jumping their rope and chanting their chants.

We were stared at for a while in silence by those outside the Alley gate. They were baffled. You could tell what they were thinking. Each was thinking maybe we *had* been up here all along, that maybe each one thought another had looked up here or climbed up here to see if we were lying on our bellies, hiding, practicing a ruse.

I smelled an advantage. From my superior position in the tree house I looked down at those at the gate and studied them from under my spectacles. I said quietly, to show how much more civilized than my mom I am, "We have not been out of the Alley."

"Timmy?" his mom asked uncertainly.

"No, Mom. No-o-o-o," he said.

I can read Tornid like a book. He was torturing himself, wondering whether *under* the Alley was *out* of the Alley or not. The moms know we—Tornid, anyway— don't lie. How could we lie to such penetrating moms as these? They might pretend to believe you and say, "I see, I see," then later on, from something they let drop, you know you have not deceived them. They are brilliant moms. But now, puzzled in spite of all their brilliance, they stood with all the others in a silent cluster watching Tornid and me winding our string balls in nonchalance.

We got the picture of what had happened, confirmed later by my *gril* sister, Star. Since there was no "us" around anywhere in the Alley, they'd asked Jane Ives. No, she hadn't seen us. My dad . . . no, or he couldn't remember. The two stranger *grils* just said they didn't know the names of everybody yet, and they chewed their gum and jumped their rope, one end tied to Billy Maloon's fence, there being only one turner. Then, naturally, the moms thought the worst—that we had gone off for another spree on the Myrtle Avenue El.

So, off to Myrtle Avenue the whole Job Lots crew had gone, to the A & P, the flea market of the blind man, all interesting places, even to the astrologer's named Madame Fatima, where we would never go, not behind the brown curtains anyway. And now, instead of being cross with us any more, they got to be cross with each other. "I thought you'd looked in the tree house." "I thought *you* had . . ." Hot and tired, they were all putting the blame on some one or another of them. However, black-eyed *gril* studied us with her impenetrable eyes. From up there in the tree house, me and Tornid looked down on the squabblers amiably.

Finally, Tornid's mom said, "Well, don't you want your Job Lots presents?"

It's a custom that the kids that don't get to go to Job

Lots, well, *they* get to have a present brought to them to compensate for having had to stay at home and not see the batch of weird remainders—garb mainly—and hear the moms' shrieks of laughter as they try on dusty items. Believe me, you'd love that store, a treasure house. So Tornid and me slid down, reached through the iron gate for our presents, and went back up in the tree house to see what they were.

You'll never believe it! What me and Tornid got in one fell swoop! Each one of us got a wrist watch—identical—that shines in the dark, has a minute hand, a compass, and tells the day of the week, all—I mean it—on one wrist watch! It must have taken all the plaid stamps of a whole year, plus the acorn stamps, too, to get these two watches. We'll never complain again about sticking the stamps in books, or anything else. We didn't even think to ask what the members of the expedition had gotten—probably some small item—we were so happy . . . and surprised!

"Gee, thank you," Tornid called down to those still at the Alley gate, and I said it, too.

"Not even anyone's birthday or anything," I said.

"I know," said Tornid. "And they could have bought an electric carving knife, even," he said. "For themselves."

"But they didn't," I said.

Those outside the Alley gate disappeared. Tornid and me hardly noticed. We were setting our watches, day . . . Saturday . . . and all. North pointed to the Empire State Building, so they were accurate. We watched the hands of our big watches slowly move. I put mine inside my T shirt. The hands shone. Tornid said he was going to stay awake until midnight to watch his change from today to tomorrow.

Consider the help that, unbeknownst to them, the moms

had bestowed upon us for our under-alley expedition! While we had been sitting in the tree house, shivering, shaking with fear over the words spoken below . . . DON'T SIT IN THAT CHAIR . . . trying to bolster up our courage with foreign French words, *Courage, mon ami,* to go down below again, see what the moms had been doing for us—buying us these neat watches that tell you everything you need to know!

Thusly had the moms steeled our *courage* for come what, come may, below.

Nerves quieted now, spirits high, we began to take stock of the tunnel knowledge we had so far, taking it in that it really existed in real life and was not something Hugsy Goode had made up or that we had drawn maps of and stored under the Ives's television.

We especially pondered about the chair and about the speaker of the words. I hadn't drawn a chair on any of my charts and plans—a chair just being there at the best central spot of the alley tunnel under the drain above. Rooms, offices, a PIT, studios, bunks in barracks for unearthly little men at war with other unearthly little men from other pits and bunks . . . smoogmen . . . I'd drawn all these. But I'd never envisioned a chair like an Uncle Ham chair with words hovering over it in tunnel air saying not to sit in it. And just before the descent, we had imagined many things that had proved not to be right. The swirling, sworling lost river, for instance. A Grand Canal with small canals, maybe, going off into narrow passageways where you'd have to stoop to get to places of business, possible to reach only by gondola. No. So far this was a tunnel that looked like the Alley on top except that it had one chair in it and a creepy voice above the chair that said words . . . in English.

Why didn't the voice rope off the chair if it didn't want anyone sitting in it? Who would think not to sit in a chair, the only chair so far, down there in the under alley? We mulled this over every which way. Then it dawned on me.

"Oh, now I get it, Tornid," I said. "That chair down there, that chair that we've named the Throne of Hugsy the Goode, was put down there when this tunnel was built, so that an antique lady like Mrs. Harrington is now, only not her, some other lady who was antique in that day and age, could rest, sit in it, then go on her way to wherever the tunnel goes."

"Goes, yeah?" said Tornid.

"Well, Tornid," I said. "What was the reason for the tunnel? And why has it been closed up, sealed up tight all these years waiting to be discovered by us, us who got the hint from Hugsy Goode that there might be one?"

"Uh-h," said Tornid. "Maybe they wanted to get out of the snow?"

I said, "You're right, Torny, old boy, old boy. You're pretty bright, and you should skip a few classes, get into some V.R.A. (Very Rapid Advancement) class and come on along up with me in Grade Six."

Tornid laughed. His eyes shone. "I got four A's, three B's," he said.

"Well, Torny, as you were saying, '. . . get out of the snow.' You ever heard of the great blizzard of '88? People still talking about it, and these houses were built before that. That's why they should be landmarks. You heard about that famous blizzard, Torny, old boy, old boy?"

"No. I was born in Arlington, Mass. 02871, on 8 Howe Street at two o'clock in the morning, and they don't talk about famous blizzards there . . . they talk about famous hurricanes. And I was born in one. It was named after some *gril.*"

I said, "Well, this tunnel was built in the age of the great blizzards, not great hurricanes. Old people and young people of that antique time could sit down there, have a cup of tea, visit with each other, sit in the Throne of Hugsy the Goode, not born yet, take turns and rest, before wending their way down the alley tunnel to where it wends. Mrs. Harrington would have been young then, Miss Land, too, another ancient lady of the Alley, a teller of stories and a foreteller of fortunes by tea leaves. They could have their cookies and tea and Mrs. Harrington wind her string amassing her fortune, and Miss Land *telling* her her fortune by the tea leaves, and they could talk or guess, maybe, how many feet the new blizzard up top would be, hope it would beat the biggest so far, the blizzard of '88."

Tornid said, "You mean this underground alley was just for old ladies to sit and wind string in? And talk? An old ladies' tunnel, not for sewing . . . my gram sews . . . but for winding string? No boys allowed, maybe?"

"Oh, no," I said. "It was for everybody. Perhaps the men, old and young, bowled, sending the balls all the way to the end . . . and the boys played miggles . . ."

Tornid said, "How did they see?"

I said, "Not gaslight. Too dangerous . . . get asphyxiated."

"Kerosene lamps?" said Tornid. "Like Uncle John's farm in Maine?"

"Too dangerous," I said. "By candlelight, cluck. Candlelight. This college has always been hipped on candles. Candlelight ceremonies . . . yop, that's it. Candlelight ceremonies are part of the past, present, and future of Grandby College. Miss Land . . . she writes poems . . .

she made up a song about it all, and they sing the candle song every chance they get."

"Don't sing it," said Tornid. "Because it's day . . . on top."

"How can I sing it, cluck! I don't know the words of it. They might have crowned the Snow Queen at Hugsy's throne, in bad weather above . . . they have to crown a new one every year . . ." I said.

"It would be nice to parade through the tunnel with lighted candles singing the candlelight song. Carols, too. Down there in the creepy dark, you don't know whether it's Christmastime or what. It's just tunnel time," said Tornid.

"Well," I said. "Now we'd know because we have the watches that tell the day . . ."

"Those were the days, though," said Tornid. "The olden days of the tunnel. Carols above in good weather, carols below in any weather, all gather in the Circle, if there is a Circle, at the end . . ."

I said, "Well, we'll find out all those things, including information about the sayer of the words, DON'T SIT IN THAT CHAIR! That sayer may have been the guy who scared the antique ladies and all the others out . . . in olden days. The Snow Queen might have been about to sit down, having been crowned by the then president, and the Voice spoke. DON'T SIT IN THAT CHAIR. So everybody fled, had the tunnel sealed up, and no more candlelight processions. Well, we have to rescue the tunnel from the voice of the chair . . . worse than ordinary smoogmen . . . may be the chief smoogman. That's what we have to find out . . . so the tunnel can be used again."

Tornid said, "You mean we really are going back down in the tunnel . . . again?"

I said, "Of course we are, cluck, and *right now.*"

"That's what I thought," said Tornid. "Because we have the watches now, and if we get caught, we will know the day . . . mine still says Saturday . . ."

A great guy, Tornid is. What other boy, aside from me, would have the courage to go down into the alley tunnel after that creepy voice saying those creepy words?

"Come on, Tornid," I said.

"Courage, mon ami," he said.

Chapter 19

The Words Again—Descent No. 2

We slid down from the tree house, and we listened. No sound or sign of the moms. Napping, probably. Job Lots expeditions are wonderful but tiring. All that strange garb the moms try on, studying which will make the biggest hit when they come home, put it on, and pay a surprise visit to Jane Ives or Cornelia Crane, Lucy's mom. Cornelia also appreciates strange garb and sometimes even goes to Job Lots with them, encouraging them to buy some dusty wig or a dress of olden times—the twenties —with fringes or feathers.

"Garb" is a real word, not one of our code words "brag" spelled backward. If you don't know what a "garb" is, look it up in the dictionary. That's what John Ives says to do when you come upon a strange word in a book. He says, "When I was a boy, I never read a book . . . all the works of Dickens, all the works of Sir Walter Scott— how I loved *The Heart of Midlothian*—without a dictionary right beside me."

So, the tired moms were probably napping or trying on their garbs, and the tiny weenie Alleyites were probably napping, too. All along we had worried about a tiny Alleyite, Holly, maybe, climbing into the hidey hole to play and falling through our entranceway into the tunnel. I told Holly there were witches under the squash vines and to pass the word along to Lucy, so they'd stay away, and they had, so far.

No sign of the main *grils,* either . . . Beatrice, Isabel, and Star. They were probably busy with whatever they had gotten at Job Lots. The only people around right now were the same two stranger *grils,* still jumping rope, and my sister *gril,* Notesy, who'd joined them. Notesy's dreamy. She doesn't know what's going on half the time, though once she did spot a ten-dollar bill before anyone else that was blowing around a vacant lot on Larrabee Street.

So, it was lucky for us it was dreamy Notesy and not black-eyed *gril* who had come out to play with the new *grils* at the rain drain, because that black-eyed *gril,* for instance—she just does not miss one single trick, no sirree. And if we had not seen her drive off with the others this morning, we would have suspected her of having tracked us, and followed us, and peered down into the tunnel glooming after us—even of having slid down behind us and spoken the creepy words, DON'T SIT IN THAT CHAIR!

Then, all day, she would have gotten that awful look on her face that means "I know something," then maybe spill it at good-manners mealtime at the Fabians' when it would be potent and be hard to contradict, say, "I know where Tornid and Copin were this morning . . ."

Yechh!

The two new *grils* have no looks, awful or not on their faces—no smile, no frown. You don't know whether they see you or not. They keep their cool and chew their gum . . . rot their teeth. And believe me Tornid and me keep our cool with them, too, because we haven't got their number yet.

All told, it was a good time for Descent No. 2.

"Courage, mon ami," I said. We jumped into the hidey hole, readjusted our gear, balls of string ready to tie, as

before, got our shillelaghs in proper position for Descent No. 2, and down we went. The descent was easier this time because now we knew how far it was to down. But it was even scarier because of the words.

Once down, we stayed at T.N.F. a while to see if the sayer of the words would come and get us or was watching us nearby. We were scared, but I said, "I see you. Come out, come out wherever you are!" No one came. We flourished our shillelaghs and flashed our lights everywhere. Then we turned our lights off and examined our neat watches. The hands were large and bright. The compass needle shone, too, and it was still pointing to where, above, north was, toward the Empire State Building. It was still Saturday.

We turned on our lights again and took a minute to admire this man-made tunnel. Now that we were getting to know it, we saw how neat it was. You could carry on business of almost any sort down here, have a store, a school with report cards, a library with hours posted when open—everything you can think of—a mush room for LLIB to grow mushrooms in. Each child could have a den. We could have a little village down here—if only that certain person, the sayer of those creepy words, hadn't gotten here first, maybe had laid claims to it, though he had not named the chair. We had. But we didn't want this Tunnel of Hugsy Goode run by some creepy voice—like a computer. That bugged us.

So, saying the magic words again, *Courage, mon ami,* we proceeded on our creepy journey to where the Throne of Hugsy Goode was located. We kept our beams steady on it. Then, I'm not kidding—ask Tornid—we saw that something was sitting in it. Me and Tornid took root where we were. We kept our flashlights steady on the whatever-it-was to blind it and so it could not see us. You can always sense when something is alive or not. This was alive, man, alive. But it was not human.

If you read as many books as I do every year, you probably have already guessed that this alive thing sitting in Hugsy Goode's chair was . . . right . . . the raccoon, the unique and, maybe, the one and only raccoon in the whole world who is as curious about the underground as he is about the upper. Probably when he looked in on me and the Fabians that night and saw how cosy it was with people sitting in chairs and eating, he thought this chair down here could be his. He sat there, looking at us from under the arm of the chair, like a raccoon king of the underworld.

The first thought that struck me was this. If a raccoon is as unnatural as this one, who likes the underworld so much he spends all his time here, sometimes sitting in this now famous chair instead of in his shaggy nest in Miss Alderman's tree, maybe he might be unnatural enough to be able to speak the human language—English —too. He *might* have said the words, DON'T SIT IN THAT CHAIR!

Wrong! Because the words, seeming to come from some presence hovering *above* the chair, like words printed in the balloons in comic books, came again—the same identical words, DON'T SIT IN THAT CHAIR! "Sit-in-that" was blurred together and sounded like one word . . . sitinthat. Then there came a counting, breathless counting . . . one . . . two . . . three . . . four . . .

"Scram!" I said to Tornid. However high up the numbers were going to go, perhaps ten—that might be the death knell for us. We didn't wait to see if the raccoon scrammed or not. We just plain scrammed as fast as we could, got up and out and back up in the tree house—our second retreat in one day from the Tunnel of Hugsy Goode.

Now, how could we ever go back down there with that creepy voice that'd said the same thing to us twice in one day? Each time it had waited to speak until we got near the chair. We should close up the hole so it couldn't get out and get us. But we didn't want to trap the raccoon down there in case this rare example of a raccoon wanted to get out, too. Cripes! Who wouldn't want to get out, be he raccoon or be he human? Cripes! Who wouldn't?

Tornid said, "It's funny that that raccoon was not scared of the words."

"Maybe he does not understand the human language," I said. "Or . . . he's mesmerized. Perhaps rattled."

We sat there in the tree house again, in glumness and in gloom. The Alley was still very quiet. Many small ones watch television at this time. But now there were five *grils* playing jump rope, being perfectly satisfied—I mean it —to play a jump-rope game hours on end, while all the time, right under them, a creepy business goes on.

They wound up one jump-rope song—the one about how many hearses will I have?—and after a rearrangement of who was turning and who was jumping, they began on another. This was a new one to me. The new *grils* must have brought it to the Alley from Staten Island, where they used to live. I'd never heard it. The words gradually seeped into me.

> "The king goes here,
> The king goes there,
> The queen goes here
> And everywhere.

"They sit on a throne,
   They sit on a chair.
   No one else can sit
   On that chair.

"Someone tries,
   Someone dares.
   Then says the king,
   DON'T SIT IN THAT CHAIR!

"How many lashes shall he have?
   One,
   two,
   three,
   four,
   five . . ."

I said, "Tornid," I said. "You half asleep while the whole plot is unfurling?"

He said, "I'm not sleeping. I'm waking."

I said, "All right. Then what are those clucky *grils* saying as they turn and jump rope?"

"They're counting," said Tornid.

I said, "Now listen carefully, Tornid. Because now, it's another *gril*'s turn."

"I am listening," said Tornid. "Carefully."

They got up to DON'T SIT IN THAT CHAIR and said it. That's what they said, all right. Tornid's large gray eyes widened. "Hey!" he said. "They been down in the tunnel. In our tunnel! I'm going to tell Mommy! They been scarin' us."

You have to hand it to Tornid with his ESP for figuring things out. Some obscure things are as clear as daylight to him, and without his knowing it, I study every remark he makes for clues or meanings I might miss. Well, that's why he's my pal—forget the age gap. So I thought over what he'd said. All the *grils* might know about us and the tunnel. The new *grils,* being new, could be the top lookout people, while the real *grils* went below. They might even have discovered a different entrance to the tunnel. They might have told the new *grils* about it to show that they were friends and not to be scared because they were new any more . . . they were in friendly territory. Neat as this theory was, I could see it was wrong, because the first time we'd heard the words, they'd all been at Job Lots and only the new *grils* had been jumping.

"No, Tornid," I said. "You're not right. The *grils* did not follow us down there. It wouldn't be as creepy if they had, but they couldn't have, what with Job Lots and all. I think I have a clue about the words. Come on. We have to go down again."

"Again?" said Tornid. "You mean to say we have to

go down in the tunnel . . . again? Three times in one same day?"

"Whassa matter?" I said. "You tired?"

"Me? Tired? I'm never tired. I stay awake all night sometimes, I'm that much never tired."

"Come on, then," I said, and we slid down the slide from the tree house for Descent No. 3.

Chapter 20

The Throne of Hugsy the Goode
—Descent No. 3

This time, for Descent No. 3, we left our string and thread behind because they were all tangled again and we didn't need them anyway since this time we planned to go only as far as the Throne of Hugsy the Goode. By now we knew that path very well, could have found it in the dark, ha-ha.

Of course, if my hunch was right about the words, we could keep on with our tunnel exploring. If wrong, back up we would have to go to consider new strategy. Anyway, the psychedelic chalk marks on the walls, arrows pointing this way and that, were more convenient than string. I threw my ball of string down to Dorothy, one of the Fabians' cats, to play with. Tornid saved his for their other cat, George, so there'd be no jealousy.

We slid down the slide. *"Courage, mon ami."* We said it together and reserved the wish we could have made for when we got back to the upper Alley—if we ever got back. This made two wishes saved in the wish bank.

"I feel creepy," said Tornid. "Twice we heard those same words."

"You won't feel creepy, soon," I said. "In a minute you'll be able to put two and two together."

"How come?" he said.

"You'll see," I said. "I hope . . ."

We went straight to the chair. The raccoon wasn't

139

there any longer. He must have gone somewhere else into the glooming, because we hadn't seen him come out of the hidey hole and return to his natural habitat, his nest in Miss Alderman's tree.

We stood back to back in front of the chair so our flashlights could be beamed in every direction. We didn't touch the chair, much less sit in it. Then, just as before, came the familiar words . . . DON'T SIT IN THAT CHAIR!

They sounded just as muffled and as creepy as before. We listened carefully. "How many lashes shall he have? One . . ." etc.

"Oh-ho," said Tornid. "It's the jumping *grils.*"

"Right," I said. "Those words are coming from the rope jumpers up there at the drain."

And we were not afraid.

"I'll sit," said Tornid boldly. "They can't lash me, because I'm down here and they're up there."

"Brilliant," I said.

Tornid sat. Then he got up. "There," he said. "I've sat in the Throne of Hugsy the Goode, and nothing happened to me."

Then I sat down.

The whole chant floated down to us. This time, from the z's, I could tell whose voice I heard. Beatrice, the black-eyed *gril.* "Don't zit in that chair . . ." she said.

Why could Tornid and me hear voices from the upper Alley so clearly through the ceiling of the tunnel that we could even tell what words were said and even who said them? Because up there on top, the drain, at last, after the big rain that created ponds in people's backyards, had been cleared out. It had been a great morning for the teeny ones—reclaiming soggy, soaked stuffed animals, rusty toys, and pieces of dolls, a lovely day with lots of loud accusations and crying and charges and counter-charges about who owned what.

Cleaning out the drain, even though, naturally, it does not open into the tunnel, helped the accoustics, and the words sounded good and loud in the tunnel. We deduced the drainpipe up top was located just the other side of the brick wall of the tunnel behind Hugsy's chair, making a good funnel for carrying voices down here.

Now that we had deduced that the creepy words, DON'T SIT IN THAT CHAIR!, had all the while been coming from the rope jumpers above, Tornid and me decided to give the *grils* the creeps.

Hoping my voice would waft itself up as clearly as the *grils'* had down, I said, at the right time in the chant, "DON'T SIT IN THAT CHAIR!"

We listened. No reaction. They hadn't heard and were up to the countdown. When the one jumping was about to say, "Nine," I shouted it. "Nine!" I bellowed.

If the *grils* heard, they did not say, "What's that?" Maybe they thought it was one of themselves. The next jumper began, "The king goes here," and so forth. Before the *gril* could say the creepy words, I said them, much louder than before. I bellowed them, "DON'T ZIT IN THAT CHAIR!" I said "zit," not "sit" on purpose because black-eyed *gril* was still doing the chanting. I'm not dumb.

Then there was silence above.

Then Black-Eyes said, "O-o-o-oh! Did you hear that?"

"I thought it was you," said Blue-Eyes.

"I thought it was *you,*" said Star.

For a while up there, there was total silence. Perhaps they were speaking in whispers which do not penetrate tunnel ceiling, pipe, or wall. Then Black-Eyes said, very loud, "We muzt have been miztaken." That was to throw creepy things off the track, like I do myself. But she will be all eyes and ears, just like me, and if . . . I never said she isn't bright . . . she drops the "z" habit, she may make it into Rapid Advancement like her sister Blue-Eyes.

Then they began chanting and jumping and counting again . . . testing, probably. Again, at the right moment, I butted in and said . . . and I spoke a little louder . . . "DON'T ZIT IN THAT CHAIR!" I resisted a temptation to say, "Don't zit in the Throne of Hugzy the Goode."

"O-o-o-oh," Black-Eyes said. "I heard it again. A ztrange hollow-zounding voiz. Lizzen."

They listened. So did we. They began to make guesses, talking in excited high voices we had no trouble hearing. "It's an echo," said one of the stranger *grils*. "I've been to Echo Lake."

"No, Marlene," Black-Eyes said. "It'z not an echo-o.

We haven't zaid thoze wordz yet. An echo haz to echo zomething, not zay it *before* you zay it."

"Brilliant!" I muttered, not to be heard above.

"I'm getting zort of zcared," said black-eyed *gril.* She is afraid of the dark, thinks every creak a burglar or an unknown something. Her big black eyes were probably growing larger by the minute and her little button mouth smaller and tighter. Maybe there were scare tears in her eyes.

We couldn't hear anything Blue-Eyes said—she has a soft voice—or Star or Notesy, and couldn't tell whether the stranger *grils* were scared or not. We haven't got a line on them yet. They might be thinking there was some sort of catch to the whole business that the others had thought of to trip them up and make them seem stupid.

"¿Quién sabe?" I said to Tornid, and the two of us basked in the contemplation of the terror above.

"We'll try it onze more, and if we hear the zoundz again, the zame wordz, I think we zhould tell Mommy," said Black-Eyes.

They began, "The king goes here . . ."

I said quickly, "The king goes there . . ." I had the sense to disguise my voice and sound like a *gril,* which made Tornid roll on the ground and cover his mouth, not to laugh out loud.

The chanting stopped. No talking. Stunned silence. I had said "there" instead of "here" so the *grils* would certainly realize I was definitely not an echo. I might be a tape recorder, but who in the Alley can afford a tape recorder, all fathers being professors, or artists, or both, and with not that much money? Or architects?

Black-Eyes spoke. "Zomeone muz be in a tree or zomewhere, maybe zpeaking into a tube, a rubber hoze, or perhapz a cardboard roll like what paper towelz come on. Zomething! Muzt be zomebody . . . you know who . . ."

Tornid and me laughed silently and slapped our thighs. We know who "you know who" are . . . Copin and Tornid, explorers of the under alley.

Up there on top there was silence again while, probably, the *grils* made a search. Then they came back, and there was more talk. Black-Eyes did most of it, and we could hear her best. "No one iz around. They are not in any tree. I don't underztand. It'z creepy."

Then someone else came along up top. It sounded like —let's see—yes . . . LLIB, Billy.

"Now zpeak the truth, Billy. Were you imitating uz from zomewhere?"

"What's that mean?" asked LLIB, who was only just four in March.

Black-Eyes explained. "Did you zay juzt now, 'The king goez there . . . ?"

"What king?" asked LLIB, his voice cracking a little.

The *grils* performed the jump-rope game and said the chant to make things clear to LLIB. "No-o-o," he said.

Black-Eyes, having one of her brothers around, even though he was only four, to give her courage, said, "Let'z try again. To make zure."

This time I let them get all the way to DON'T ZIT IN THAT CHAIR! and I put it in again ahead of them.

LLIB said, "You did it. You said it."

Billy has to be on guard, too, like new people, because he is only four and likely to be tricked.

"No, Billy, I didn't," said Black-Eyes.

"Then one of *them,*" said Billy. He probably meant the new *grils*.

"We didn't," they said.

"Oh-ho-ho," said Billy in a confidential tone. "I know who said those words."

"Who?" came the chorus of *grils*.

"Jimmy Mannikin," said Billy.

"Who's he?" asked the *grils*.

"A little man that lives down there. Wakes up every morning, wakes us up pounding on the pipes, sending up steam—fixes things that need fixing . . ."

"Oh," said the *grils*.

"Ye-ah," said LLIB. He was warming up to tell a huge long story. He likes to tell long stories, and takes his time telling them. "Jimmy Mannikin goes where he has to go, where his work takes him. Sometimes he lives down there. Sometimes he runs along the telephone wires in the country. He carries messages and sounds, zoomy, zoomy, zoomy. Ay-and, if you put your ear to the telephone poles, you can hear him, going zoomy, zoomy, zoomy . . ."

"Oh," said the *grils*.

"Ye-ah," said Billy. "Ay-and, I asked Jane Ives . . . she told me about Jimmy Mannikin first . . . is he real? Ay-and, she said, 'I spose so, because I made up him.' So he's real all right. You just heard him. Only . . . I never heard him talk before. Only just banged the pipes before or went zoomy, zoomy, zoomy on the telephone wires. Never heard him talk before. Good-by! I'm getting out of here."

That was all we heard from LLIB.

Now, tired of this part of the tunnel affair, me and Tornid decided to get on with the exploring, leave the *grils* to their confusion and creeps about the creepy voice *they* had heard. Served them right for giving us such a scare in the beginning.

Tornid said, "They didn't mean to scare us. They

didn't know we were down here. They don't know anything about the chair of Hugsy Goode."

Tornid has not learned yet that you can't, you just can't be nice to *grils*. They will take advantage of you, some sort of advantage . . . don't ask me . . . *any* old sort of advantage that comes along . . . every time.

So, coping with our own creeps about the unexplored and main part of the maze which, seen from here, from the Throne of King Hugsy the Goode, our home and safe place, stretched on and on into the glooming, we set forth, shillelaghs held high, to wherever on and on might lead us.

"Courage, mon ami," I said.

"Oui," said Tornid. *"Bon ami."*

I appreciated the wit but did not laugh.

Chapter 21

On Down the Alley Maze

My brand-new watch that shone in the dark told me the time, day, and direction—four o'clock, Saturday, May 22, and N. still pointing where it should. We had at least an hour and a half before horn-blowing time; and the day had not switched over to Sunday. If it had switched over to Sunday, we would not have been surprised because it's like being in another world, being down here. We were facing up the main part of the tunnel, which, up top, faces south—S., the Circle end. And we were about to set forth into the glooming.

Weather is always the same in the tunnel. There wasn't a barometer on my watch, so we wouldn't know what it was going to do up top. But Tornid and me don't care about the weather anyway. Unless it's pouring or there's a blizzard . . . doing something unusual . . . me and Tornid almost never know what it's doing. "What's it like outside?" That's the first question grownups ask when you come in. Tornid and me have more on our minds than keep a track of what it's doing out every sec.

What we have to keep track of now is the number of steps we're taking.

"Don't talk," I said, though Tornid had said nothing. "I'm counting steps. After every five, we'll stop and take stock, be sure we're not being followed or spied on. One, two, three, four . . . five." We stopped.

"I wish," said Tornid, "that we'd come upon what you

147

drew, some of those little bunks and those little men sleeping in them in dens and places . . ."

"Those are secret places and not to be found or searched for until this main tunnel is well known to us, and anyway," I said to Tornid, "I'd rather a human skeleton, even forty of them, than live little smoogmen from Mars."

"Yeah," said Tornid. "We wouldn't know their language."

It was dark and it was creepy. This may be a fine man-made tunnel, but it sure gives you the creeps to be down in it and take steps in it into the glooming. "Forget it," I said to myself. "Think of the fame! When Tornid and me tell everybody about the tunnel, what they're going to say! They're going to say, 'That Copin! (Lots of Alley people know our aliases now—we have accidentally let them slip out.) That Tornid! We always knew they had it in them.' "

You know how people are! After a lifetime of complaints about you, and bellowing at you, and hard smacks . . . they end up saying with a proud chortle, over their coffee and cigarettes and bursts of laughter about somebody or other, "Hm-m-m. Yes . . . well . . . we always knew they had it in them." I *hope* they'll say that and not, instead, put us back into solitary confinement.

"I hope they will," I said.

"Yeah," said Tornid. "But . . . what did you say?"

"Where's your ESP?" I asked.

"Not working in the tunnel," he said.

"If we get to have our pictures in the paper because of discovering this tunnel and having it accepted into the landmarks association of New York, I am not going to take my eyeglasses off for the picture. No sirree. That's what Star does. Takes her glasses off every time she has her picture taken. Not me. My eyeglasses are part of my face," I said.

By now, counting steps, I figured we'd passed my house on top and must be where, next door to us on top, Mrs. Harrington's house is. Tornid said, "We should have brought the string. It is safer in mazes, tunnels, and forests to have string or white pebbles, even crumbs to show the way back."

Tornid's voice sounded little. I spoke harshly to him to reassure him, prove that life, even though being lived right now in the alley tunnel, was still normal. "Whassa matter?" I said. "What do we need strings or pebbles for now any more? Crumbs! Crud! Now that we have this watch with a compass? That's all we need to get back . . . right? And we have psycho chalk, too . . ."

"Yeah," said Tornid. "More up-to-date than string."

We walked slowly on, flashing our lights all around, not to be taken by surprise by something. "Wonder where that nutty raccoon is," I said.

"Maybe he thought DON'T SIT IN THAT CHAIR! meant him, and he ran and hid," said Tornid.

We walked on. It was two minutes since we'd left the chair, we were going that slowly. Jane Ives and the moms should see how slowly we are walking . . . we usually are running. "You'll break your necks," they say.

Tornid said, "You'd think we'd be somewhere by now . . . even to another chair, or something . . . a bed. It seems like we have come farther than the whole distance of the Alley, the good old Alley up top."

"Things seem further in the dark," I said. I realized, though, that I'd forgotten to count the steps after the first twenty-five. The first goof I'd goofed. But I thought we must be near Jane Ives's house on top, by now. "You still have your chalk?" I asked. I felt in my pocket and found mine.

"Oh, yeah . . ." said Tornid. "We can draw arrows," he said. "IN and OUT. Or something. Arrows to the chair."

"Right," I said.

He got his neat piece of psychedelic chalk out of his pocket and drew an arrow on the wall and labeled it IN. I drew an arrow pointing backward and labeled it OUT. Cool! The letters were phosphorescent. His shone with a spooky yellow-green color in the glooming and really looked like words written by someone from some other place. Mine were bright pink.

"Draw my name on my forehead, Tornid," I said. "In case I get lost, you can spot me. My name 'Copin' will shine in the dark like neon lights on Times Square."

He did this. "Stop wrinkling your forehead," he said. "C O P I N." He spelled it as he went.

Then I wrote T O R N I D on his forehead. We both shone in the dark now like the words written on the wall did. We zigzagged our lights across our faces, and our names seemed to wiggle on our foreheads, seemed to dangle in the tunnel darkness as though not connected to us. We turned our lights off, and all Tornid could see of me was my name, and all I could see of him was his name. It was eerie.

"'Better than string, eh, Tornid, old boy, old boy?" I said.

"More up-to-date," he said again.

"This is a modern journey in a modern maze, not an ancient one like Theseus had to find the Minotaur in," I said.

Then I drew a scary face on the wall. It shone. Whoever invented this chalk invented a neat thing. I wrote our names on the wall, too, and the date. "They may come and find us in a hundred years, if we get lost," I said. "Kids digging in the ruins may find us. Bones then, just bones, and end up in a museum with a label . . . Brooklyn *Puer sapiens. Puer* means 'boy,' *sapiens* means 'wise,' " I explained.

"Spanish?" he said. "Poor sap?"

"No," I said. "Latin. I learned it from Star."

We went on. "Copin," said Tornid. "Where are the skeletons? Not the poor sap type, the real type."

"Oh, we'll get to them," I said. "Don't you worry. And it's pu-er sap-i-ens, not 'poor sap,' lug."

I turned around. We could just barely see the Throne of King Hugsy the Goode from here, just a blur of the name over it. We should have written it in larger letters. I couldn't get that chair out of my mind. There it was. Every time you looked at it you thought someone, some guy invisible or not, some phantom, might be sitting in it and studying us as we went on into the glooming . . . just two small Brooklyn boys . . . one age eleven and the other eight on a historic journey.

I said, "Tornid, the skeletons are probably in the large pit under Jane Ives's house, a really central spot, according to my map. Those skeletons may have been there all of our lives, Connie's life, too, and would be there until doomsday if that boy, Hugsy Goode, had not said there probably was a tunnel under the Alley. It's too bad he's grown up and moved away and gone to college. I know he'd like to know he was on the right track when he said those words . . . be part of this expedition."

"Yeah . . . I know," said Tornid. His voice was shimmery, like his name on his forehead. And on we went into the glooming.

We must have passed Jane Ives's house by now. We didn't stop to see if there was a crawling or narrow passageway to it from the main stem of the T. First we had to find out if there was a Circle. We went straight on ahead to where it should be, if there was one, under where the Circle on top used to be.

"Tornid," I said. "If it's skeletons you want, you have to look in every direction . . . we don't *know* they're lopped all together in the PIT under J.I. Don't think you're just going to come upon a skeleton grinning at you and saying, 'I'm here.' You have to look."

"I didn't know skeletons could talk," said Tornid. "Maybe the poor sap type can, but none I ever heard of could talk, not the ones in museums. They never say anything. Grin—that's all—and I hope that one knows not to talk. Just because he's in a tunnel, not a museum, he might think he can . . ."

I stopped, stood stock-still. "What's that you said?" I asked.

"I just said," said Tornid, "I hope that one doesn't talk. Maybe you are looking for a better one—one that will say something."

"What are you talking about, cluck?" I asked.

"I'm talking about that one back there," said Tornid.

"What one? Back where?" I said.

"In that pile of stuff back there," he said.

"I didn't see any pile of stuff," I said.

"I did," said Tornid. "And it looked like a skeleton in it. Maybe he wasn't any good . . . no good at all, probably."

"Show me," I said. Suddenly my knees grew weak. Tornid wasn't scared . . . too young to be.

Tornid flashed his light to "back there." By cricky! There was a long bone sticking out of the rubble with what looked like a big bone toe on it sticking out, too.

The rest of him, if there was any rest of him, was in the rubble . . . thank goodness!

"Come on, Tornid," I said. "I'm getting out of here."

I ran down the tunnel, passing the IN and OUT signs, past the psychedelic face wobbling at me horribly—I wish't I hadn't drawn it—past the Throne of King Hugsy the Goode, down the Fabian tunnel to T.N.F. and our rope.

"Wait for me," said Tornid.

I waited. I boosted him up and out and hoisted myself out, too. There we were then in clear air, not heavy dark, dank skeleton-infested tunnel air. "Whew-ee!" I said.

And thusly ended Descent No. 3.

"Why were you so scared?" asked Tornid. "It was only a part of a skeleton, not a whole one with a grin. So, why were you so scared?"

Chapter 22

Meanwhile, What Had Been
Going On Up Top?

What's so scary about just a piece of skeleton? I didn't know, so I didn't answer Tornid. All I knew was I was shaking. Tornid began to shake, too, because shaking is catching. We wobbled out of the Fabians' gate to resume life with human beings, hostile though they might be, and not live life in a tunnel with skeletons, whole or in pieces.

We were not met with any hurrahs because all the kids, about ten of them, lay flat on their stomachs, looking like spokes of a wheel, around the drain which was like the hub. Their heads were as close together as they could get around the drain that carried sounds down into the tunnel and, vice versa, carried sounds up. How ignorant the spokes are! They did not know that, although the drain was just an ordinary drain, it was very close to an under-alley tunnel.

Standing outside Fabians' gate, Tornid and me studied this human wheel a moment. Then I put my fingers to my lips, meaning be silent. Then, unobserved by the drain watchers, we jumped over my fence, over Mrs. Harrington's fence, over Jane Ives's fence, over the Arps' fence, and climbed up the Arps' tree.

Then I bellowed at the spokes, "What's up down there?"

Without relinquishing the spot that each spoke held, they turned their heads toward us like turtles.

We jumped out of the tree, sauntered back down the Alley, hands in our pockets. "What's up?" I said. "You hearing the voice of the boogeyboo?"

They passed around a look that meant, "Play it cool."

Tornid said, "Yeah, what's up?" And he laughed his funny hoarse laugh.

"Or . . . down?" I asked. I looked down at the spokes from under my eyeglasses.

Tornid's huge gray eyes were sparkling. "Yeah!" he said. "What's down?"

We had broken our rule not to speak to *grils,* but we had made our secret non-contamination sign and were temporarily safe.

"Oh . . . nothing," said black-eyed *gril,* a strand of her long brown hair in her mouth.

Blue-eyed Izzie just sniffed.

"Move over, someone," I said. "What's going on? Some new corny game?"

LLIB said—his eyes were round and brown and very serious—"We hear voices. We hear words."

"Well, let us in on it," I said.

LLIB said, "They told me it was you. I said, 'No, it's Jimmy Mannikin.' And I was right."

"Oh-ho-ho-ho-ho!" I laughed. "And there we were, Tornid and me, up in the Arps' tree!"

We ran away then. Exit laughing.

"Ha-ha," said Tornid. "We fooled them."

What a success our words from the underground had been! We couldn't stop laughing. Our tunnel terror was over. The skeleton leg that had terrified me seemed funny now, too, and we laughed remembering its big bone toe. But we had to figure out about the skeleton. So we went over to Jane Ives's house, where we do a lot of our figuring.

On the way Tornid said, "You s'pose to tell the police when you come upon a piece of skeleton?"

"Not unless it's a whole one," I said. "Maybe we'll come upon the rest of him, or even forty whole ones like they did down in Brooklyn Heights."

I couldn't help it, I began to get the creeps again thinking about the piece of skeleton. Tornid wasn't at all scared. I'd told him there might be skeletons on the tunnel trip, not to be scared, and he wasn't scared. He thought it was OK for there to be skeletons in a tunnel under an Alley where people live, go about their business, have potlucks, and such, blow their cow-horn blasts, swing, jump rope, have visitors—all this going on on top of a piece of skeleton. "Anyway, it wasn't like those whole ones that time in the FUNNY HOUSE you come upon suddenly," said Tornid. But I didn't know what to think.

"Let's ask Jane Ives," I said. "We should have excavated and found out if there was more to him than the leg and the toe."

"Get that next time under," said Tornid.

Shucks! Jane Ives's back door was locked. We looked through the Alley gate. Yop. The old gray Dodge was gone, so she and John were off somewhere, not just Jane over to Myrtle Avenue to do the shopping stint. The theater maybe . . . they like to go to the theater.

So that was the end of telling Jane anything yet, and the secret of the tunnel and the skeleton remained just Tornid's and mine. Just as well. I still wanted to surprise Jane when the whole exploration of the tunnel is completed—knock on her door some afternoon when she was cooking dinner, say, "Jane. Hugsy Goode was right. There *is* a tunnel under the Alley. So far, it's as we drew it on some of the maps." Have her say in total surprise . . . drop a spoon, perhaps . . . "Copin! I wondered where you and Tornid were lately . . . no new pictures on the door gallery . . ." Explain then. Explain the whole neat thing and hold her enthralled. That would stoppeth her in her tracketh and never mind she forgot the Worcestershire sauce for my tomato juice.

We sauntered back to the drain. Life under the Alley was scary. But life on top was tame. The drain watchers and listeners were drifting away, the mystery of the words below still unsolved by them . . . just as before, the mystery of the words from on top had been unsolved by Tornid and me. Tornid and me had solved ours, though. Ha-ha! One up on the *grils.*

At the drain, just Notesy *gril,* Blue-Eyes, and Black-Eyes were still there. "Whatcha listening for?" I asked. "A conversation between . . . uh . . . two skeletons?"

Tornid and me laughed vulgarly.

Blue-Eyes said, "Skeletons don't talk. They are silent."
To back her up, Black-Eyes said, "They do not have vocal chords."

We sneered at them.

Then we went back to the hidey hole. "Maybe we should board up the entrance so no one will get suspicious," I said.

"Yeah," said Tornid. "And steal the leg, maybe even the chair of Hugsy Goode . . . hey, and maybe even write other things on our wall . . . bad words . . ."

But we didn't block up the hole because of the raccoon. He might want to come out and remind himself of the stars. Anyway, just then the cow horn blew, and I had to go home. "It was a long day's night," I said.

"Yeah," he said.

"See ya," I said.

"See ya," he said.

I went home whistling, "It's a long day's night," because that's what it had been like down in the tunnel all right. I whistled softly, though, not to rub my mom the wrong way. I still felt grateful for the neat watch bought with all those stamps.

My mom was in a good mood because she had found garb she liked at Job Lots. What a long time ago that seemed . . . yet it was just this morning. "What kind of garb is that?" I asked.

"You'll see," she said. "Bayberry got one, too."

"Looks guru," I said.

"They're abas," she said.

She laughed thinking of the stir she and Bayberry Fabian would create when they paid surprise visits on their friends in the Alley in their abas.

I was in a good mood, too, and washed my hands without being told. What a day . . . mark it on the calendar!

I did. On the big kitchen calendar I marked T.F. People would think that meant Tornid Fabian. But it meant, "Tunnel Found."

A whiff of what my mom was cooking in the oven made the day just about perfect. Barbecued lamb breast. One good thing you can say about my mom is she is a very good cook, and this dish is a specialty of hers. If your mom has never cooked that, brother, then I'm sorry for you, that's all.

Everyone was in a good mood and no one yelled at anyone. Notesy told the story of the voices that came up out of the drain. But she is not a good storyteller . . . it's from fear that people, me and Steve, might sneer. The story did not create a ripple. Star was not home. She was having dinner with the Fabian *grils* or she could have put in her two cents, having been one of the spokes also. My dad tried to listen to Notesy. "Really!" he said politely. But you could tell he had his mind on something else, the new Grandby president, probably.

After dinner I went up to my half of my room to catch up on writing this book before Steve came up. Things were happening thick and fast, and I had to get them down . . . like that piece of skeleton coming in right now . . .

"Now, Racky (I began addressing my remarks to the raccoon . . . it's my custom to talk to someone, even a raccoon, when solitary), don't go moseying around the skeleton bone. That's Tornid's and my skeleton, our pet one."

Pet skeleton. So, what's so funny about that? Some places they shrink heads, have a shrunk head for a pet. Cripes! The things people do!

Tomorrow, when Tornid gets home from Sunday school, maybe we can get to go down in the tunnel again

—that would be Descent No. 4—and dig out the rest of that skeleton. Usually, there *is* more to a skeleton than just a leg and a toe. I wasn't scared any more, my mind having decided he was a pet. And my new watch was shining in the dark beneath the sheets, on my wrist still.

See ya.

Chapter 23

Words from Below Again

If you think those spook thoughts last night about skeletons kept me awake the entire night, forget it. They didn't. I never slept better. It gives a guy a nice feeling to find that something—the under alley—almost exactly, except for a few additions, exists as I had drawn it.

I went out in the sunshine . . . it was early in the morning. The Fabians were at church, and there was a Sunday silence in the Alley. While waiting for Tornid to come home, I went over to Jane Ives's, what I usually do Sunday mornings. She was in the kitchen and was waiting for someone, John Ives or Connie, to get up for heaven's sake so she could get to work. She paints.

Sundays, while we wait, she and I chew the fat, and I have a little second breakfast. Today I had sausages—four—English muffins—two—two doughnuts, four prunes, and some non-coffee coffee. A nice snack. I made a list of it all to show Tornid. When Jane opens the refrigerator—it's a game we always play—I reach my hand in from under the door and take out an egg from the shelf on the door.

"Surrealistic," says Jane, seeing just my hand and the egg. I have never dropped one. And Jane has never said, "Careful . . . you might drop it!" She trusts me—just says, "Surrealistic," seeing my hand and the egg.

I kept wanting to tell Jane all about the tunnel so far.

161

But I held back because Tornid and me wanted to surprise her with the whole thing. Then, I'd say, "Jane. It's all true, as I drew it." Lead her down there and say, "Behold the Tunnel of Hugsy Goode!"

I sat down at the dining-room table and drew a new and complicated maze. Then I looked at the art gallery on the cellar door. Two *grils* had drawings there. And they were good . . . I have to say it—to you, not to them . . . they were very good. Black-eyed *gril* had drawn a cat on a fence and Blue-Eyes goldfish in a tank. But they took up too much space and made me grumpy. There was hardly room for my new maze.

In a while, Tornid came in, hair wetted down, face shining and clean. Don't worry. My face was not dirty either. I'm not that crazy about dirty faces and hair. No one has to hold their nose when I pass by even if my hair is long like Oliver's. I . . . all of us . . . do take a bath every day. Just like the Fabians. Six of us, five of them—not counting the moms and the dads—adding up to eleven baths a day.

In the water shortage Mr. Frank Fabian put the three boys in the tub together. My mom didn't believe in that. Each of us six, shortage or not, had a bath . . . skimpy, but a bath. No wonder John Ives clasped his head the day of the Larrabee Street River and shouted in despair, "Consider! All that water gone, gone, racing away." And he had to go to Coney Island and wash in the sea. He said he did. My mom said, "Yechh! In that water?"

Tornid had some tomato juice, and then we raced out. "See ya," we said to Jane Ives, who closed her eyes tight not to see us when we broke our necks, if we did, going down the steps. We latched her gate so Atlas Maloon couldn't get in and scruff up the grass and the garden— John Ives has one of the prettiest in the Alley. The

Maloons don't care. Many people besides John Ives complain. "Why can't they walk their dog outside the Alley like decent people do?" they fume.

"Tornid," I said. "You think there's time to go down under before lunch for the descent numbered four? Nothing to be scared of . . . I don't know why you were so scared . . ."

"I wasn't scared . . . you . . ."

I looked at him and he didn't finish. "No," I said. "Nothing to be scared of. What's a piece of, just a *piece* of skeleton? No grin. Is he worth being scared of? And there aren't any spook voices any more, saying not to sit. We know those voices came from the *grils*. On top."

"Yeah," said Tornid. "Or us below."

"First them, then us," I said. We climbed the Arps'

tree to take stock. The Alley was quiet. Where was everybody? Contamination Black-Eyes, where was she? Contamination Blue-Eyes, the two stranger *grils,* where were
they? Everybody? Where were they all with their jump-
rope games, their "King goes here, Queen goes there,"
their "Here we go round the mulberry bush" with the
teeny ones while baby-sitting?

Only us, Tornid and me, were out.

This made the Sunday silence seem more silent than
ever. Creepy, too, knowing what we did of the tunnel and
its piece of skeleton including toe.

Usually, Sunday mornings, which are not Job Lots days,
or A. & S. specialty days, are the times for moms' relax-
ing, for chatting over the back fences, for strolling into
one another's backyard, mug of coffee in hand, beginning
with how tired they are—a few words here, a few words
there, some laughter; gaiety amongst the grownups, the
dads gardening or in the cellars, talking about what's new
at college, admiring or studying new paintings, or sculp-
ture, making frames—just chewing the fat.

When you think of it, Sundays are really nice days here
in the Alley, good smells coming from the kitchens,
chicken or roast pork, sometimes, *grils* and others doing
what they want—practice, homework. Some prefer doing
homework the minute they get home Friday so it's done
and out of the way. I don't. I do it on the way to school
Monday morning to get the gist.

But now, nobody was in sight.

"Where is everybody?" I said.

"I dun-*no* . . ." said Tornid.

We swung out of the tree and checked. My grownups
were in the cellar, a landmark in the Alley—it has so
much in it. My mom retrieves every possible thing that's

any good at all from what gets thrown out of the Engineering Building opposite us—even from the trash cans along Larrabee Street. We have some neat things . . . a real slate blackboard, four feet wide by two feet high, they'd just plain chucked out over there.

Tornid's mom was down in our cellar, too, with her mug of coffee. Well, that was something natural going on. But it beat us where everybody else was. LLIB, for instance, where was he? Tries to stick around with us whenever he can. Not now, though.

"A ghost Alley," I said.

"Yeah," said Tornid.

"Well . . . no reason to be scared," I said.

"I'm not scared," said Tornid. "I'm never scared, unless I have to be."

But an uneasy feeling began creeping over me.

I said, "Whoever created that skeleton or that piece of one out of a bygone man, well that guy might have figured how to coax all the Alley children down there and make skeletons out of them, hoping to surpass the record of the forty on the Heights. Right?"

"Right," said Tornid. "In one of the offices down there we haven't found yet."

"A sort of studio," I said, "for the creating of skeletons."

We're not crazy about the Contamination *grils,* but we don't want them skeletonized. Nor Danny and LLIB. Not even the two stranger *grils* whom we don't know very well. We might be the only survivors among the twelve-year-olds and under.

"Should we tell someone that all the children are lost? Even tell them about the tunnel?" I said.

"I dun-*no* . . ." said Tornid.

At the drain where, yesterday, we had seen all the *grils* together, all of them alive, flat on their bellies, all lying together, heads touching, legs fanning out, like spokes of a wheel, listening for the words from the bowels of the earth, *our* words, though they didn't know it, now, around the drain, nothing . . . no body. The bare arm of a little doll poked in by Holly, maybe, stuck out of the drain. We got it out and set it on the curb. Was the little doll a sign . . . was the skeleton-maker at work? The drain held us in a spell. Gooseflesh popped out on me. If we ever see the *grils* again, we'll quit the C. game . . . and we'll let LLIB and Danny play with us all the time.

"Where is everybody?" I said. "Think, ya crud."

"Maybe they all got dead," said Tornid.

"Yechh," I said with a sudden reversal of opinion. "They have discovered the secret of the tunnel. They've found the entrance, gone down there without any invitation from us, the true tunnel finders. Probably down there right now, the whole slew of them, squealing and gasping, 'Oh-oo-ooh!' I can hear them in my mind, and see them . . . maybe having a torchlight parade . . . weeny ones on the big ones' shoulders . . . planning a circus down there . . . something. . . . Yechh!"

I kicked my foot against the cement curb in bitterness.

Tornid caught it. "Ye-ah," he said. "Those *grils* . . . they spoil everything."

"Serve them right," I said, "if the skeleton-maker does find them. We do the work . . . they get the fun. They'll tell everybody. And it's our tunnel, ours to tell about."

"We should have named it after us, not Hugsy Goode."

"Can't. It's already been named, written on the walls in psychedelic chalk," I said.

We lay down and put our ears to the drain. "What do you hear?" I said.

"Just you, breathing," said Tornid. "Don't breathe your breath in my ear," he said.

"I know what I'll do," I said, and I did it. I said the jump-rope chant. In high *gril*-like breathless tones I spoke the now famous words. When I got to the line, DON'T SIT IN THAT CHAIR!, I paused.

And, before I could say them, up from the bowels of the earth came the words, eerie and muffled . . . DON'T SIT IN THAT CHAIR!

"Cripes!" I said. "That proves it! The *grils are* down there . . . one of them probably sitting on the Throne of King Hugsy the Goode! Maybe even have one end of their jump rope tied to it . . . no respect for ancient objects. Come on, Torny, old boy, old boy! We'll get a jump rope so we sound more authentic, say the whole thing, and listen. See if they say the words ahead of us like we used to do to them, see if they put the line in just like we used to do, see how talented *they* are . . . the copycats!"

We tore to my house, went down in the cellar, got one of Star's beat-up old jump ropes, and tore back out with it.

Knock me flat! My gosh!

How'd they get out so fast? There, gathered around the drain again, spokes of a wheel again, were all the *grils* and some boys, all with ears to the ground, not all dead in one fell swoop or saying words below.

"Where ya been?" I asked. This was the second time in one week I had spoken to *grils*. Blue-Eyes just looked at me. Her lips were pressed together in a I-won't-cry position. I think there were tears in her eyes. Black-Eyes spoke. She said sharply, "My dad drove all of uz . . . us . . . over to Myrtle to get the Zun . . . Sunday paper. And popzick . . . sickles. (She is trying to break herself of the 'z' habit . . . her father will give her a quarter if she does, Tornid told me.) You think you're so smart, don't you? We know what you did . . ."

"Sh-sh-sh . . ." said LLIB.

Silence.

"Bee-cause . . ." said LLIB, his ear to the ground. "We heard voices again. Yes, we heard them again . . . just now . . ." His voice squeaked a little . . . it does sometimes.

I said, "Don't give us that Jimmy Mannikin line again."

"He's not," said Black-Eyes indignantly. "There *are* voices below . . ."

"Oh, yeah?" I sneered. "Let's hear them then. Don't hog all the space."

Blue-Eyes stood up and stepped aside. There *were* tears in her eyes, about to brim over. But she held her lips tight together and did not cry out loud. I felt embarrassed for her. And I flopped down on my belly in her spoke space. Tornid squeezed in beside me.

We listened. Cripes! We didn't know what to think. Here were me and Tornid on top. And instead of the *grils* being down below, discovering, *invading* our tunnel and saying the words we had heard, here all they had been doing was going off in the Pugeot to get the Sunday paper with their father! Cripes! It used to be they on top at the drain, and us below, imitating. Now . . . who was do-ing the imitating? Cripes! There came the words again . . . DON'T SIT IN THAT CHAIR!

I looked at Tornid. I said, "Tornid, I bet you don't hear anything. You take a swot at this best place here and listen."

Tornid listened real hard. His eyes grew wide. It was clear he heard words. "I bet you don't hear anything," I said. "Do you, Tornid?"

I pressed my elbow into his ribs and repeated, "You don't hear anything, do you, Tornid? I don't."

Tornid crossed his fingers under his belly and said, "No." This way he knew his lie was a white one and would be forgiven even if today was Sunday. He doesn't lie very well. Even I don't. I only lie to protect my rights . . . my rights being Tornid's and my claim to the alley under the Alley with all its skeletons, lost rivers that had really gotten themselves lost, Throne of Hugsy the Goode, even eerie voices, the tunnel with all its mysteries still to be solved.

"They must be deaf," said Black-Eyes. Blue-Eyes was still unable or unwilling to speak. "Deaf as a post," said Black-Eyes, right ear to the ground and piercing me with her impenetrable eyes.

The two new *grils* pivoted around on their elbows and looked at us without any expression at all. Black-Eyes said to one, "Marlene. You hear those words, don't you?"

New *gril,* Marlene, nodded and turned her gum around to the other side of her mouth so the saliva would not slide out with her face turned sideways. That was all.

"What did you hear *it* said?" I asked sarcastically.

"Oh. You can listen," said Black-Eyes. "Maybe *this* time you'll tell the truth. Maybe your ears have cleared up by now."

I was curious. If it was the skeleton-fellow, I had to know so I could recognize his voice if I heard it again, not mix it up with the jump-rope *grils* on top, when we got down there . . . if we *would* go down there again. I listened. This was what I heard.

"Testing . . . just testing . . . stand by . . . testing . . . Roger . . . do you hear . . . testing . . . Roger . . . DON'T SIT IN THAT CHAIR . . . for Pete's sake . . . Ay ah . . ." Then, in a deeper, really hollow tone

. . . "Tee-ornid . . . Co-opin . . . where are you? . . . Testing . . . testing . . ."

My eyeballs nearly fell out of my sockets. Tornid had heard, too. Who could miss his own fake name spoken in that creepy voice coming out of the depths? We didn't miss it, neither of us did, but we didn't say ah, yes, or no.

"Well . . ." said Black-Eyes angrily. "You must have heard all that, didn't you?"

"You've all got bats in your belfry," I said.

"And you've got them in your ears," she said.

"Aw," I said. "You all give me a pain." I gave several of them shoves to show how pained I was, and they all rolled over like dominoes. "Come on, Tornid," I said. "Let us leave the little ones to their little game."

Blue-Eyes spoke. A real tear was rolling down her cheek. She quavered, "What did you do with it?"

"Oh, never mind them," said Black-Eyes. She put her arm around Blue-Eyes and gently led her away whilst whispering in her ear.

"What's she talking about? What'd I do with what?" I asked Tornid.

"I dun-*no,*" he said.

We adjourned to the tree house, where we could keep our eyes on the hidey hole and see if anyone came up it or went down it, and where we could puzzle about this new slant. It began to look as though someone else *was* down there, imitating the whole bunch of us, *grils and* me and Tornid, and even saying, "Tornid . . . Copin . . . where are you?"

Cripes! Our aliases!

Chapter 24

The *Grils* Accuse Me

Sitting up there in our . . . Tornid's . . . tree house, puzzling and puzzled, I asked Tornid, "How many *grils* are there in the Alley?"

"About . . ." said Tornid.

"No 'abouts,' Tornid. Be accurate, cluck! And by *grils* I mean real ones, not tiny future ones like Holly and Lucy."

I counted them up out loud. "Your two sisters, my two . . . makes four. New *gril* 1 and new *gril* 2 . . . makes six. Bird, a *gril,* though not often here, but visiting the Fabians because it's Sunday . . . she makes seven. And all of them are around the drain right now," I said. "Seven around the drain."

"Like the seven sisters in the sky," said Tornid.

"Yeah," I said. "Except that these happen to be seven sisters of the under alley. The up-top *grils* may not only have aliases like we do, but they may also have other selves, smoog-*grils* that impersonate them. . . . Or," I said, "maybe the full-grown *grils* up here are training the tiny ones, Holly and Lucy, to slide down our entrance-way, go into our tunnel, and squeak up their voices . . ."

"Like a Fagan . . . seven Fagans . . . training two little tiny girls to become *grils* . . ." Tornid said.

"Well, still," I said, "I really don't think so. The *grils* are kindhearted at base toward tiny ones. Besides, Lucy had the chicken pox."

171

And there was little Lucy, her pale face pressed against the windowpane of her little back bedroom window looking longingly out at life. So, who was making a mockery out of all of us?

At the drain the *grils* began to jump rope again and say the same old chant, which gets on my nerves now as much as the dumb music of the ice-cream man on Myrtle . . . diddle-de-diddle-de-dump-de-dump. Yechh! It's enough to turn you against ice cream. You could tell the *grils* were not having very much fun. Often, before the person was counted out, they all plopped down and listened for the voice from below. From our high place you could see one or the other nod her head as though to say, "There, there it is again."

I said, "Torny, old boy, old boy. The *grils* are just as goofed up as we are."

"I'm not goofed up," said Tornid. "I just think they're the voices of the smoogmen. You drew plenty of them . . . their offices, bunks, dens, and everything we haven't come to yet. But we will because so far everything is the way you drew it."

I have respect for Tornid's ESP and listened.

He went on. "If there are smoogmen, there might be smoog-*grils* and smoog-moms to cook and keep house. They imitate real good," said Tornid. "They sound exactly like real *grils* above the earth and like me and you."

"Well," I said. "We do have to consider everything . . . smoogmen, women and *grils* . . . space ones. They may have flown a saucerful of them down last night, or even long ago. They may have set up housekeeping then, long ago, in the days when people held tea parties in the under alley, scared everybody out so they'd never come back and they'd have it to themselves and their business. They may be sending messages back to their smoogmen base about things they've heard from on top, like us being on their trail with our shillelaghs and psychedelic chalk; they may study the meanings of all this, whilst all we want is to just plain explore a man-made tunnel and not interfere in the least with smoogmen or the life they lead and their wars, if they war. They may think the *grils'* jump-rope chant is a special signal like we did. They may have eaten the rest of that man, that skeleton, leaving the leg bone for later because probably they eat bone, too. . . . If I didn't know that Hugsy Goode was alive and a student with a beard at Mich. State, I'd think, I might think that that leg bone . . . it's a long bone, and Hugsy, they tell me, is very tall . . . might be . . ."

"Cripes!" said Tornid. "If there are little spacemen or smoogmen down there eating college boys, I'm never going down there again. They may eat small boys, too."

"Don't say 'never,' Tornid," I said. "It's a bad thing to say 'never.' "

Then Tornid said, "Copin. Maybe raccoons do talk after all. He's the only alive thing besides us we know goes down there . . . and him being a sport raccoon?"

"Oh, cripes!" I said in disgust. "Same old theory."

Then, suddenly, the way *grils* do, they all hopped up and said, "Bye," and, "See you later." Some went down the Alley to where the Circle used to be. My sisters went into our house, and the Fabian *grils* came into their yard. They didn't look up at us, in the tree house, and we didn't look at them. We kept our eyes on the hidey hole, and they didn't go anywhere near it or even look at it.

They stopped on the top step of the back stoop. Black-Eyes said, loud, meaning for us to hear, "Where do you think your mini tape recorder is, Isabel? It is not in the dray-ain. The Commodore let us take off the lid and feel around, and it is not down there. Yet we hear it from somewhere below. Nicky is bad, Isabel. But, one thing I am sure of, I am sure he would not steal anything as important as a mini tape recorder that you saved up for by collecting all those wrappers from Highlander's Paper Towels, going from this house to that in the Alley getting people to save their Highlander wrappers for you, even asking Miss Hogan at P.S. 2 to change her brand of paper towels and save the wrappers, even though they cost one cent more than some other brands. And all those who do use that brand did save the wrappers for you, and it took you five months to get enough to send away and get your mini tape recorder. No. Nicky would not steal anything as ex*pen*sive as that. A piece of gum, maybe from, say, me or from Jane Ives's back porch at trick or treat time. But, a tape recorder, a mini tape recorder, *your* tape recorder . . . no!" Her black eyes flashed at me in the tree house.

Izzie Blue-Eyes sniffled. Bravely holding back her tears, in quaversome tones, she said, "But who? I loved my little tape recorder so. It would have made a timeless accurate historical record of people in the Alley. I would ask permission to tape a person so I would not get them making bad remarks about someone. I would not be violating their constitutional rights. I was getting real neat things, like . . ."

Unable to continue, Blue-Eyes groped her way inside, Black-Eyes protecting her from behind, guiding her as one would a person shocked by some piece of very bad news. They made me feel guilty. I didn't know what they were yapping and sniveling about . . . they had me stumped. Then they must have changed their minds and got mad at me all over again, because back to the door they came again, and Blue-Eyes, tears running unchecked down her cheeks now, said, "Timmy. Nicky. You stole my nice new mini tape recorder and threw it somewhere, some secret somewhere, and it is going on mini-taping itself, and it will ruin itself and it will ra-a-ain!"

Well, that shook me up. I shouted, "I didn't even know you had a mini tape recorder. So how could I steal something I didn't even know the existence of? Why didn't you show it to us if you have one?"

Black-Eyes, still standing on the top step, arm raised, finger pointed at us, said, "Because we knew you would steal it. And you did!" And she added, "And, *Copin!* (She had heard my alias and used it now to show that 'Copin' was the Mr. Hyde of *Dr. Jekyll and Mr. Hyde* . . . Nicky being the Dr. Jekyll.) We know that you put it in some secret place. We hear it. You heard it, too. Yet you said you didn't. I saw you cross your fingers, Tornid. (She

used his fake name, too.) So . . . you not only steal
. . . you do not tell the truth!"

Back into the house Blue-Eyes went to fling herself, I
supposed, face down on the divan and let sobs wrack her
and tears swamp her and not watch television either.

With one last lethal glare, Black-Eyes wheeled around,
slammed the kitchen door and went in, probably to com-
fort her sister with whom she sometimes disagreed. But
not now. The two were united now in hatred of me and
Tornid, especially me, being three years older and hated
three times as much, leading Tornid into doing such
things as taking a mini tape recorder from his sister and
going over to Myrtle Avenue that time.

Well!

I said, "Tornid. I didn't even know blue-eyed *gril* had
a mini tape recorder."

He said glumly, "Me neither." He was shook up because he had been left out of common Fabian family
knowledge.

"So. How could I steal it? Anyway, I don't steal. How'd
they get that crummy idea?"

"They just don't think you are any good," said Tornid.
"You reapeth what you soweth," he said.

I was shook up and insulted. I don't steal. I earn my
money. And I earn my money in much harder ways than
minding small children or saving Highlander's Paper
Towel wrappers. My money me and Tornid earn, we earn
by collecting, saving, and tying up old newspapers. They
are heavy, believe me! Everyone, almost, in the Alley
saves them for us, and we put them in my cellar, and we
tie them up, and once a month we put them in our blue
bus and my mom drives us to Goodwill Industries and we
get one cent (1¢) a pound for them.

I felt grumpy. I decided to resume calling *grils* "Contamination" loudly, not silently, whether the moms liked it or not. I looked at Tornid. He was staring at his house, and he looked miserable. Maybe even he, my pal Torny, old boy, old boy, suspected me, too. I asked him.

"You crazy? Cluck!" he had the courage to say.

Well, Tornid *knows*. He *knows* I don't go around stealing things, not unusual things like mini tape recorders, especially. Once, a piece of crumbly old chewing gum from Jane Ives's porch, an ancient stick from trick or treat days, and I had to spit the crumbs out because it would not stick together.

Then Tornid said, and he looked me straight in the eye, "You know . . . raccoons *are* thieves. They may not talk, but they *are* thieves."

Then the light burst on me, on both of us. Of course! The facts suddenly became clear.

Fact 1. Blue-eyed *gril* had a mini tape recorder that we didn't know about until now.

Fact 2. It was missing.

Fact 3. Raccoons are thieves.

Fact 4. Last seen, Raccoon was sitting in the chair of Hugsy the Goode, down below in the under-alley Alley. . . . Where he'd gone to after that, we didn't know.

Fact 5. *Grils* know our aliases now, had even called us by those secret names on tape. How much more did they know or would know soon?

So, next chapter, please.

Chapter 25

Descent No. 4 or Nighttime
in the Tunnel

We would have gone right back down there for Descent No. 4, but we had to have Sunday dinner then, me in my house, Tornid in his. I was still shook up about the *grils* having accused me of having done something I hadn't done. The only thing worse than being accused of doing something you haven't done is being accused of doing something you have done. Then you have to face the music. But I had no music to face, and I ate my dinner . . . oven-fried chicken . . . and I thought about the new twist in the tunnel affair.

What Tornid and me had to do was we had to go back down as soon as possible. But after dinner Tornid had to go with his entire family to visit his gramma. He didn't get back until after supper in the evening. I was waiting for him in the tree house. His mom turned on the television right away, and they were saying still no settlement to teachers' strike in sight. Tornid joined me in the tree house. We felt carefree.

"You know what that means, don't you, Torny, old boy, old boy," I said. "No teachers, no school. Even though it's Monday, tomorrow . . . no school."

"Yeah . . . " said Tornid. "Neat."

"So, here we are, Torny, old boy, old boy," I said, "being handed a present of another day off by the teachers who usually can't stand it if you stay out one single day and spoil the gold star your room might get for perfect attendance . . ."

"M-m-m," said Tornid.

"So, Tornid," I said, "since you and me are going to stay out until at least nine o'clock, maybe a little later if the moms are in a jolly mood and there's joking and coffee under the grape arbor, how about we—you know what —we go down into the tunnel?"

"Nighttime . . . in the tunnel?" said Tornid.

"Sure," I said, as though that's when we always went down. "What's the sense of being any more scared to go down in the nighttime than in the daytime? It can't be any more nighttime down there in the nighttime than it is in the daytime. What's the difference?"

"Same difference," said Tornid. But he looked worried.

"You know, Tornid, we may turn out to be heroes if we not only locate the entire tunnel, but also find the missing mini tape. Then we could proclaim a truce and end the war between the *grils* and the boys."

"Hey, yeah," said Tornid.

I could see he was pleased at the idea of a truce. Sometimes he is in a bad spot figuring, when he's out of my sight, how to react to *grils* that happen also to be his sisters.

"Well, we'll see," I said. "Anyway now, down there in the nighttime, we'll have a chance to unwind some of the threads of the story of the under alley, the lost mini tape recorder for one . . ."

"But," said Tornid, "we don't use thread or string any more, now we have psychedelic chalk, so we don't have any to unwind."

"Not those threads," I said. "The plot threads."

"Mommy will miss me," said Tornid. "She'll whistle and I won't answer. Everyone will miss me. They'll count us up . . . two girls—I mean *grils*—and three boys. But there will only be two boys. My dad will say, 'Bath time, boys.' He always collects the boys. And there won't be any *me* for my bath."

"Oh, bath time," I said. "Forget it. We'll get back in time anyway, I think. Remember what you said. Before dinner, you made an important remark . . ."

"About . . . raccoons . . . the robbers they are?"

"Ye-ah," I said. "Probably that raccoon has come up top more often than we thought. Probably did steal Blue-Eyes' mini tape recorder and took it down into the under alley, liking the sound of human voices, even taped ones."

"Hey . . . yeah," said Tornid.

And it was all go-Roger with Tornid, now. We got out our paraphernalia where we keep it, in the rain-proof sack under the squash vines of Hugsy Goode. We looked at our watches. Seven-thirty. As we prepared to leave the upper Alley, it was twilight time and no stars were out yet. But soon it would be nighttime, above. And we, below in the under alley, would know if nighttime felt any different than daytime.

So I said, "Down we go, Torny, old boy, old boy. Now beginneth Descent No. 4th. The usual order, first me, then you."

Getting down was sure easier than it used to be, we'd scrambled up and down so many times. It would have been neat if we could have taken the slide off the tree house and fixed it in the entranceway. It's just about the right height. Then we could slide down and in . . . skip the rope. But the slide would have been missed. When the great day came and all could be revealed to young and old, then the grand tour of the tunnel, with the mayor coming along also perhaps, could commence with a slide down the chute . . . whee-ee!

Now, once down, I said, "See, Tornid? It's no darker down here than it is when it's broad daylight up top. Pretend that it's afternoon out, instead of twilight time with darkness approaching and the seven sisters soon to come out . . . up top in the sky. Say to yourself, 'It came a little early, night did, tonight.' "

We stood beside the letters T.N.F. shining beside us. "Yeah," said Tornid. "But I used to like to see daylight slanting down from the hidey hole when we came back, when we used to take daytime trips."

"Never mind, Torny, old boy, old boy," I said. "We're really going to have fun now. Better fun than they used to have in the good old days of the Circle."

We went as fast as we could to the Throne of King Hugsy the Goode. Soon, by the light of my flashlight, we saw two little round beady eyes staring at us. Though I knew it was the raccoon again, I jumped behind Tornid and said, "Don't be scared."

Tornid said, "I'm not scared. It's just Racky, just like before . . . same eyes."

"I know it," I said. "He likes that chair. More comfortable than a tree. Probably why he stays down here so much."

As we drew nearer, the raccoon looked at us curiously . . . not afraid. When we got to him . . . yes sirree . . . Tornid's ESP was right. There *was* something between his paws, and it *was* a mini tape recorder! Right now the recorder wasn't saying anything. It had played whatever was taped on it out. "Testing" was the last word we had heard from above. I hoped the tape was not all used up because I wanted to add something.

I stood beside Hugsy Goode's throne. I didn't reach for the mini tape recorder because, although raccoons are tame, how'd I know about this particular one that likes staying in a tunnel instead of a tree? He might think that because he had stolen this mini tape recorder it was his, and he might bite.

I said, "Racky?" I spoke very gently, the way the Fabians speak to pets. "How would you like to have your voice recorded?" I asked. "For the landmarks records of the tunnel?"

Racky didn't say anything. He just jumped down and ran away to somewhere . . . wherever he likes to go in this tunnel that he probably knows more about than Tornid and me do so far.

We examined the mini tape recorder. It was neat. Best of all there was still room on the tape for more words. I told Tornid, "Once I get the thing working and we've heard the last recorded word . . . 'testing' . . . you say something, Tornid. Say, 'Coming, Mommy.' That's in case she calls you."

Tornid laughed. He said, and I taped it, "Coming, Mother. Yes, Mother. Yes, Mother. I hear you, Mother. Where am I, Mother? Here, Mother. No, not in the Arp tree. Here. Right here, Mother. Home in a minute."

Like this, if his mom called while we were down here, she'd hear the message, and she wouldn't worry. "But," I said, "why'd ya say 'mother,' cluck? You always call your mother 'Mommy.' "

"I just thought," said Tornid, "that because it was on tape, it should not be the same as real life."

"Cluck," I said.

But we left it that way, and it sounded neat. We filled up some more of the tape in this reassuring way, and I hurled a "Whatdya want?" in after Tornid's words in case my mom was shouting "Nicky (me)" or blowing on the cow horn.

Tornid and me pictured the two moms saying, "Why! Did you hear that? Why, where in the world are they?"

Well, Tornid and me had a real laughing jag—the first one ever in the tunnel. It was a wonder we didn't split our solar plexuses. But suddenly we stopped. We grew sober as we realized that now we had to get on with real business—the questing and the exploring of the tunnel.

"How do you think Racky got hold of Blue-Eyes' mini tape recorder?" I asked.

"She leaves everything around . . . maybe left it on the back step a minute and the next it was gone. Can't find her glasses or her spelling book most the time," Tornid said.

I thought that some day, if the *gril* and me ever got to be friends, I'd ask her where she'd left her mini so's Racky could steal it. I wouldn't ask for a reward if I returned it to her . . . especially for returning something she had the nerve to think I stole. She almost had me thinking I had stolen it in my sleep or something.

We set the tape recorder carefully on King Hugsy's chair. We felt safer than before, having touch with the upper Alley this way. We set it going and had another laugh at Tornid's voice. "I squeak," he said.

"The acoustics are good down here," I said. "Imagine a drum down here, or a band . . . a bongo band!"

"Ye-ah," said Tornid. He liked listening to himself on the mini tape recorder and hated to leave. He wished he could sit on King Hugsy's throne and play his words over and over again. But there was work to do whether he was tired or not.

"Come on, cluck!" I said. "We have to go!"

We pushed the button that set the mini tape recorder

talking away again from the beginning, only now it had added onto it its special and reassuring message to the moms in the Alley above. Then we stepped forth again, into the glooming. "Coming, Mother," the recorder said, while we went the other way.

Chapter 26

On into the Glooming Again

About to set forth, I looked at my watch. I made a note of the time—seven forty-five. We should try to get back by nine-fifteen. That was just about as late as the moms were likely to be content with the "Coming, Mothers." We hurried on to where we had located the skeleton leg . . . fifty paces. This time I'd remembered to count. There it was . . . it had not been bothered. I wrote on the wall beside it in psychedelic chalk, Speciman A. "Pretend it is a beef bone leg, and it won't scare you," I said. "I'm sure it's not the leg of Hugsy Goode. We would have heard about it if he'd disappeared."

"I never was scared," said Tornid. "And I don't think a skeleton without a head is a very good one."

"Are you crazy?" I said. "Even just the toe would have been valuable, even just a plain footprint of a skeleton is better than nothing. Everything means something . . . a clue to olden times. Look at museums . . . filled up, some of them, with bits of skeleton. They take them home, the diggers, and imagine what the whole guy might have looked like, then display him in a case with words they think explain what age he lived in, give or take a million years."

We dug around the crumbled wall with our shillelaghs, but we couldn't find more of the guy nor a trace of crockery that would tell what age it lived in. I drew a picture of a head of the guy on the wall, marked Speciman A, with grin and sockets, not realizing how spooky this was going to look. We couldn't erase it, though, and went on again into the glooming.

Far and straight ahead, my light shone on another wall —probably the end of this main passage of the under alley, the long end of the T. Was there a Circle or not? That was what we wondered. We hurried up there. There was! There was a Circle just like the one they used to have on top. Tornid had never seen that one.

"This one is just like it," I said.

"Hey," said Tornid. "Neat. We could get our bikes down here, ride around down here, like they used to do on top."

"*¿Quién sabe?*" I said. "In the old days down here, they might have had a round stage in this Circle, a theater like in the days of Shakespeare . . ."

"Neat!" said Tornid. "But I'm not going to act in it if they do that again. LLIB and Lucy can, not me . . ."

"You can be a stagehand," I said. "Or blow a trumpet at the right moment."

We went back to Speciman A, easy to spot by the scary face I'd drawn. We examined the wall opposite it. We knew that on top we would be outside Jane Ives's garden gate because of the fifty paces paced from the drain above and the throne below. There was one place in the wall that was darker than the rest. We focused our lights on this place . . . it was a void. "Torny, old boy, old boy," I said. "That isn't just wall opposite this skeleton leg. That's void. There must be a passageway there."

We stepped across the tunnel. There was an entrance . . . no door . . . into a passageway, narrower than the main tunnel, about half as wide but just as high. Like the T.N.F. passageway, it was not a crawling-through tunnel, I'm sorry to say. "Torny, old boy, old boy," I said.

"This passageway must be under Jane Ives's house . . . or between it and the Arps'. Now . . . to see where it goes."

Outside this passageway, on the main wall, I wrote J.I.—IN, with an arrow. Inside of it, I wrote OUT. We were not taking chances on getting lost. So far, this tunnel has not been as involved as some I've drawn and hasn't even had any crawling-through passages. But they may show up. We're on the watch and we're on our way, on into the narrow passageway of J.I., not knowing what perils may be behind or ahead of us, on our way to somewhere.

We counted our paces. We took twenty. We must be very close to the house of the Iveses up top. It made us feel safe. If we said something, we wondered if she would hear. I said, "Ja-ane. Jane Ives. We're down here. Tornid and me, Copin. In the tunnel alley, at last. Look at the map on the cellar door. We are in the very spot named J.I."

"She might be in the kitchen washing dishes," said Tornid.

We tapped the ceiling of the tunnel with our shillelaghs. Maybe she would say, "What's that?" Drop a piece of china, maybe . . . make John Ives rant. Or, maybe she was down in the cellar, closer still to us, ironing. Well, we had no way of knowing, there being no drain down here to serve as a hot line between above and below.

We didn't have much time . . . it was now eight o'clock . . . and we should have gone on down Passageway J.I. right then. But wondering about whether Jane Ives had heard us or not, and wondering about the moms, whether they had heard our voices on the mini or not, made us hurry back to the Throne of Hugsy the Goode. Just plain curiosity.

Maybe on top they were all listening to what the lost

mini tape recorder was saying. They must have figured
out by now that me and Tornid's voices were on it. The
grils must be saying, "We told you so. They did steal it!"
Yechh! Not true. Used it? Yes. Stolen it? No. Besides, out
of our paper-collecting money we would pay them for part
of a new tape. They better not erase our voices from the
tape. We had to preserve them for the under-alley archives.

Back at the throne, there was Minny (we decided to
call the tape recorder Minny now, as though she were one
of the *grils*) going along very nicely. "Coming, Mother,"
etc. After my "Whatdya want!" she stopped.

We listened. No sound from above. We couldn't tell
whether anyone had heard or not. Maybe they were so
mystified, they were struck dumb. Then . . . a voice.
Tornid's mom. "It bugs me, Latona (my mom's name).
I know that was Tornid's voice I heard. But where are
they? And what's this business about 'Mother'? Tornid
must be sick, calling me 'Mother,' not 'Mommy.' "

Then Beowulf (another one of Tornid's mom's nicknames) gave her piercing whistle that involves no fingers.
A boy she knew in high school once, on the team, had
taught her how to whistle that way . . . no fingers involved, just teeth and lips and tongue. Tornid can do it,
too.

"You whistle, too," I said to Tornid.

Tornid whistled . . . very well, too, considering we
were in tunnel atmosphere.

"Did you hear that?" exclaimed Tornid's mom.

Everybody up top was so excited, we had little trouble
hearing them.

Then my mom, she whistled, the way she does . . .
puts two fingers in the corners of her mouth . . . loud.
It's enough to break your eardrums. Then she blew a blast
on the cow horn. Then silence, as they listened. Then Jane

Ives . . . she'd joined the gathering at the drain . . .
said, "Funny. I thought I heard them just now. They must
be somewhere around. You don't think . . . ?" And then
she was silent.

We trust Jane Ives. She is the only one besides Tornid
and me who knows about our maps and plans. So far she
doesn't know we've been down, though. Still, the in-
credible truth might be dawning on her. We don't think
she will tell them her hunch until we say to . . . not unless we never come back, of course. And you can see that,
to a grownup, to have the tunnel be real and not imagined would be hard to take in, even for Jane. But anyway, Tornid and me had to get on with the expedition before they did get wise.

Meanwhile, we had been adjusting Minny, and now we
started her off at the very beginning again, so she should
run quite a while and continue baffling the upper world.

Then back into the glooming we went as fast as we
could to the J.I. entrance. "They might," I said, "if they
have any sense, send Sasha out on a find-Tornid expedition,
give her one of your old sneakers to get your scent real
good and tell her, 'Find Tornid, Sash! Good dog, Sash!' "

About to turn the corner into the narrow J.I. passageway, I flashed my light back to the Throne of Hugsy the
Goode for one last look at it, at Minny, and maybe Racky,
our only ties to the upper Alley, for who could tell where
this small tunnel might go? My flashlight is a good one, but
fifty paces is far. I did see the chair all right, though dimly,
and dimly I saw . . .

"Tornid. Get inside the J.I. passageway," I whispered.
"Quick! Did you see what I saw?"

"Ye-ah, who was it?" asked Tornid, shaking.

Someone was sitting in the Throne of Hugsy the Goode!
And we heard words, not the words of the mini tape, not

the voices on the mini tape, a hoarse voice too far away to be distinct. Was the voice saying, "Get out of here!" or, "Get *me* out of here?" Quite a difference! We didn't wait to find out. We hurried down the J.I. passageway into the unknown. We could not go back by way of the chair. Now we *had* to go where the tunnel went, wherever that was.

"Who *was* that?" asked Tornid. "The skeleton-maker?"

"Sh-sh-sh," I said. "Save your breath. You may need it. And anyway, I don't know. Cripes! Why didn't we stay where it was nice and safe on top and wait for the ice-cream man?"

It seemed as though we had been going through this narrow passageway for miles. We might turn up under the Navy Yard, or even the East River. This narrow tunnel might lead right straight to a dumping place where people who had been murdered could be slid into the river and never be heard of again.

That skeleton leg might have been part of a whole man,

once intended for the river, and only the main part of him made it there. Yechh!

I was scared to turn my flashlight on behind us. At least we didn't *hear* anything or anybody coming creeping along behind us, hadn't so far anyway, and I muttered, *"Courage, mon ami."*

The words gave Tornid courage. He said, "This is not as scary as the tunnel in the Funny House where you were *always* coming on things . . . not just one bone and one man."

"Maybe he's a phantom," I said. "If we can't get out this way and *have* to go out that way, we'll chalk our faces up real scary, say weird sounds, teab ti, teab ti, hit him with our shillelaghs . . ."

All of a sudden we came to a slight bend in this tunnel. We had been coming west and now it was N.W. And suddenly we came upon a great wooden door! Cripes! It might be the door to the slide to the river, the dumping slide. We listened. No sound of water.

"There's a sign on the door," I said. "If it was a door leading to Davy Jones's locker, they wouldn't have labeled it."

The sign was old and tarnished brass. I spit on it and I made out the words: MEMORIAL HALL. "It says," I told Tornid, "Memorial Hall."

"Memorial Hall!" said Tornid. "Oh, now I get it . . . here's where we find the skeletons . . . maybe more than forty. Like 'Temple of the Dead' in olden days. Funny. Our trip on the Myrtle Avenue El ended up in a cemetery. And now this trip is ending in a temple of the dead."

"Cripes, Tornid," I said. "Don't you even know what Memorial Hall is . . . at Grandby College? It's the hall where we go to see plays and old movies, lots of things the students put on."

"Oh, *that* Memorial Hall!" said Tornid.

"Yeah, but how to get in," I said, "before that guy on the chair gets wise to the fact that we may be slipping from his clutches, his plans—whatever they are."

Then I remembered the long and rusty key. "Hold my flashlight," I said to Tornid. I got the key out of my gunny sack. It fitted in the lock. But both the lock and the key were so rusty, I couldn't turn it. My hands were trembling. I was nervous about that guy or phantom last seen sitting on Hugsy Goode's chair. He might have dropped the key in the rubble beside TRATS on purpose for us to find. He might have seen us pick it up . . . he probably has eyes that pierce the darkness . . . and anyway he could have seen us and our flashlights disappearing in the J.I. passageway.

"See if you can turn it," I said to Tornid.

While he was trying, I got my screwdriver, nail file, and jackknife out of my gunny sack. Tornid couldn't turn the key. I took it and scraped away some of the rust from it and from the lock.

"Spit on them both," I said to Tornid. "Because of your ESP, you may also have powerful spit."

Tornid didn't have much spit because he was scared, but he spit all he had. Then I put the key back in the lock. Slowly, it got to turn a little. Then it turned all the way. I turned the heavy knob, and the door creaked open toward us. Then, with a groan it suddenly swung wide open, as though someone inside had given it a push and said, "Come on in."

I flashed my light around, and there wasn't anyone there that we could see. But we were in a large passageway now, as wide as the main under-alley one. I took the key out of the lock, but I didn't lock the door in case we had to go back this way in a hurry, guy or no guy on the throne. On the wall I wrote, "To J.I.," with an arrow pointing behind us.

Key safe in my pocket, we closed the door and went on. I felt the walls. The wall on our left was warm. "Feel this wall," I said to Tornid, and he did.

"Hot," he said.

"Right, Torny, old boy, old boy," I said. "That's because on the other side of this wall is the Engine Room, where, at this very minute Orville Nagle may be polishing his old steam whistles, getting them to work for Commencement Day, or petting his stray cats. Yes, Torny, old boy, old boy. We are now in the lower depths of Grandby College. We have come through the under alley, through the J.I. passageway that's so long it stretched under Story Street, under the Engineering Building, under part of the Mall to here—Memorial Hall!"

I felt like an archaeologist discovering a site.

We went as fast as we could down this wider passage, stopping only once in a while to draw an arrow on the wall and a giant footstep on the floor, the way the students do on the sidewalk in Library Park on Founders' Day. And then—we came to another door. So we were going somewhere. "Where's this one to?" I asked.

"I dunno," said Tornid. "We didn't come to these on the maps."

"Nope," I said. "We have to make additions when we get back."

The same key fitted this heavy door, and the lock was not as rusty. Tornid had accumulated some more spit, and I said, "Spit your powerful spit."

He did. The key turned easily and the door opened. I put the key back in my pocket.

"Keep your foot in the door," I told Tornid. "There's no sign here. And you know you always have to keep your escape route open."

Tornid did.

We went in. We took a look around. We didn't need our flashlights here. A dim electric light bulb dangled from the ceiling and lighted the scene.

"Guess where we are, Torny, old boy, old boy?" I said. "Not the river . . ."

"Not the chute for sliding in the dead . . ." said Tornid.

"Not Mike's art store . . ." I said. "Come on . . . guess. The li . . ." I was giving him a clue.

"Uh . . . the-e-ah . . . library?" he asked.

"Righto," I said.

"Who's that over there?" whispered Tornid, pointing into the shadows. "Sitting on that box?"

We ducked behind a crate of books and waited.

Chapter 27

Where We Were

My heart sank. If that guy sitting on the Throne of Hugsy the Goode had eyes that could pierce darkness, he probably had a way of getting here ahead of us . . . by a crawling-through, not discovered by us yet, type of passageway where the smoogmen are. For a minute Tornid and me crouched low behind our crate, and we didn't look out. Then I figured that if he was the guy on the throne, he could see us through the wooden box anyway, so I stood up. Now he could see the top part of me with his plain eyes and the lower part with his see-through-solid eyes. I looked at the guy over my nonshatterable eyeglasses. He was asleep! Or pretending.

I studied him a second. Then I saw who it was—a man named Tweedy who rakes leaves on the campus and closes up the library at night. He'd come down here for a little snooze, probably, before ten when the library would close. He half opened his teary eyes when I told Tornid who he was, and he closed them immediately. Not interested, or maybe he thought he was dreaming.

So here we were then, unscathed, in the basement of the library of Grandby College. By way of tunnel, through darkness and dangers, known and unknown, we had landed ourselves in an old familiar haunt. How did we recognize it? Because we've been down here. The librarian, Mr. Amos B. Belcher, a friend of my dad's, gives us permission on rainy days to come down here to look at old

Popular Mechanics so we can draw pictures of old cars and make models of them when we get home. There they were now, on a shelf, dusty and tied up in batches of twelve.

We have sat here, right close to this very door we have just come through that leads from tunnel to tunnel and back to the Alley and to our beginning, T.N.F., TRATS, and the hidey hole. That was before we had the sense to take in the importance of the words of Hugsy Goode— that there might be an alley under the Alley just like the one on top. But now, we have proven that Hugsy Goode was right and deserves having the tunnel named after him, and the chair. Maybe someday he'll come back and visit and have a chance to sit in it. If he ever does come back and if that guy Tornid and me saw sitting in the chair was not a mirage and is still sitting in it, Hugsy can say to him, "Don't sit in that chair, it's mine. And I go to college."

We couldn't take time, now, to examine any of the interesting things down here (they keep the best of everything in libraries in the cellar, like people do in houses— we do anyway). Besides, we didn't have permission. So we tiptoed past Mr. Tweedy, who slept on, and we tiptoed up the marble stairs to the main floor. The library was still open, students coming in and going out. Instead of going right out, I had the brilliant idea of borrowing two books from the children's collection. We each took one, not even looking at what they were, and took them to the desk to be stamped. They were our alibi, proof we had been in the library.

The man at the desk was a student—his name is Stan —and he lives in the Stuarts' attic. He recognized us, and he did not ask what we were doing over there at this time of night—it was a quarter past nine—and he charged the books out to us. We said, "Thank you." He did not answer.

That is a privilege when you get to be nineteen, not to answer and say you're welcome. Showing the lady at the turnstile our books, that they were stamped with this day and year, we went slowly, but twice, through the turnstile to act natural, like kids, and went out.

Here we were then, in out-a-doors nighttime—the seven sisters visible now in the sky—having come all the way from Tornid's hidey hole through Hugsy Goode's tunnel and ending up here on the library porch named the "Canterbury Porch," a copy of one that's over in the real Canterbury, England. John Ives said so. He'd seen it. So had Jane and Connie. All had seen the real porch.

Then with our stamped-out books we tore across the Mall to Story Street. You can't get into the Alley without going through one of the houses, and we didn't have a front-door key. We could have climbed over the Alley gate, but we'd be seen, and anyway we wanted to come in through a front door to make our alibi, the library, even more convincing than just the books, which we might have borrowed earlier.

So first we hid our shillelaghs and other gear in the thick ivy outside Jane Ives's house to pick up later. No one answered her bell. So we knocked on Mrs. Stuart's door. She is one of the nice mothers . . . lets us climb her catalpa tree; even lets us walk across new-fallen snow in her yard now that her sons are too old to care whether or not they have first whack at it.

Mrs. Stuart came to the door and seemed surprised when she saw us. It was late for kids, Tornid especially, to be outside of the Alley. She looked at us suspiciously, the way people in the Alley usually look at me, Tornid, too—because he is my pal.

"Do you mind if we go through your house?" I asked. "Locked out," I said.

"OK," she said. She followed us to the back door. "Been to the library?" she said.

"Yeah," I said. No lie. It was true—see the books?

We went out.

"Thank you," said Tornid. All Fabians always say thank you, sometimes two or three times.

We locked her gate behind us without being asked to, so Atlas Maloon couldn't get in her yard. Then we sauntered down the Alley, books in hand that we had just borrowed from the library . . . anyone could see that—they had Grandby Library stamped all over them, with date taken, date due, the rules, etc. . . . Well, we had a foolproof alibi where we'd been. Ask Stan Woodard, the student at the desk who'd stamped us out. Not over to Myrtle Avenue, no sirree, or other forbidden places. So, up the Alley-oh we sauntered to the drain, flooded by the porch light on Billy Maloon's house that lights up the Alley right and left and straight ahead.

In this flood of light, we saw that practically everybody was there at the drain, the moms, the dads, the *grils,* big and little people. It looked like a ceremony of some sort, ancient druid times, because, for a laugh, the moms had donned their Job Lots garb, their "abas," they called them. That word aba is a real word in the dictionary and means (I'll save you the trouble of looking that word up) a long, loose flowing robe . . . neat. The *grils* were all flat on their stomachs again, like the same old spokes of a wheel. Our two moms were bent over them, heads cocked, listening. We came up behind, joined in, unnoticed. We listened to the words that held them enthralled. "Coming, Mother. Coming, Mother . . ." over and over, the whole recording ending up with . . . "Get me out of here!"

"The voice of the phantom," I whispered to Tornid. "It

really was a phantom, not a mirage. And it knows how to reset the mini tape recorder."

"Yikes!" said Tornid. "I'm glad we got out," he said, and went and stood beside his father, who was standing nearby and talking to my dad.

Maybe, I thought, we hadn't been missed. This happens sometimes. Not so. My mom turned around. She looked at us and she took us in, books and all. She pulled on her right ear—she has long earlobes and pulls on one when puzzled. "Well," she said. "There you are! Where've you been?" she demanded, the sight of us safe and sound making her mad.

Tornid's mom took the cue . . . they follow each other closely. One mad, both mad. And vice versa. "Yes," she echoed sternly. "Timothy! Where were you?"

Jane Ives was there, and she looked puzzled. But she didn't say anything. Mr. John Ives was away at a conference, or he would have explained everything, made it up if he didn't know. My mom kept pulling on her earlobe. You could see she was trying to make it all out.

I wondered if right then and there I should reveal the secret of the tunnel because I was scared about the phantom who could get out at TRATS if he wanted to. I didn't know how to begin. The moms' strange garb threw me off, and I still wanted to restore the mini tape recorder to Blue-Eyes . . . be a double hero, discover of a tunnel and recoverer of Minny. I waited while I thought what to do.

Tornid's mom said, "You boys look as though you'd seen a ghost . . . or heard one. Come on, now, where've you been?"

The flattened-out *grils* stood up. Contamination Blue-Eyes looked bewildered. Contamination Black-Eyes fixed us with her penetrating scrutiny. Then says Contamination Blue-Eyes (you remember that all Fabians are honest and fair even when it hurts), well, Blue-Eyes says woebegonely, as though now all hope was gone . . . she says, "We were wrong, Beatrice. They are not down there, wherever *there* is, with my mini tape recorder. Someone else stole it, someone who says scary things."

Well, Black-Eyes, she said nothing. Since Tornid was a Fabian and born honest, she could not say he had lied about the mini tape recorder. Yet she smelled a rat. It was confusing, even to ourselves, hearing ourselves from down below there, we knew where, though no one else did—and all the while ourselves being up here, alive and well and in the flesh and with two books stamped out a few minutes ago from the Grandby Library if anyone cared to look.

The *grils* did. They looked at the books, examined the dates minutely, and passed them from hand to hand. We saw what the titles were for the first time. Mine was named *A Little Girl's Helpful Hints on Helping Mother*. ("Retrogressing," I heard Bayberry mutter, for it was in very large print, and the *grils* snickered in spite of themselves.) Tornid's book was a wow! *Journey to the Center of the Earth*. Tornid and me were stunned at the coincidence, and Tornid's mom looked proud. "A fine book," she said. "And I'm sure you can read it. If not, I'll read it to you."

There the books were all the same, never mind the names, stamped out with today's date on them, and "Fine 2 cts. a day if not returned in 2 wks." Well, Tornid and me didn't have to say anything. The evidence was evident.

I looked at all the people through the lower part of my nonshatterable eyeglasses. There was silence except for the words from below—GET ME OUT OF HERE, and HELP! HELP! SOMEONE PLEASE HELP! I took advantage of everybody's confusion and said nothing, not that I wasn't pretty confused myself at those hoarse words that kept saying themselves over and over. "Bad as the old days of DON'T SIT IN THAT CHAIR," I told myself.

My mom said . . . and in her garb, she looked even bigger . . . "Nicholas! What do you know about Isabel's tape recorder?"

Sternly, Tornid's mom echoed, "Timothy? What do you know?"

Right then and there, I was really practicing in my mind how to begin. Tornid and me might have seen it was fitting and proper—a large part of the population being assembled—to make the revelation, lead the throng, young and old, down into the under alley, lead them in solemn procession, candlelights and all, yet give them a thrill—scare the bee-jeebies out of them with that phantom sitting in the Throne of Hugsy the Goode, amusing himself with Blue-Eyes' Minny, making fools of us all, but—the way things happen! You think you're going to do one thing (I had my mouth open to begin. . . . "Well," I was going to say, "you remember the time Hugsy Goode said . . ." and swing into his prophetic words), but then something else happens . . . so fast . . . and you have to do something else.

A bell rang. And when I say "rang" I mean "rang!" Our front doorbell! You can hear it as far away as Jane Ives's tea kettle, probably over to Myrtle Avenue. My dad went to see who it was. I waited for him to come back so's he'd be present to hear my news. I'd make it flat . . . a tunnel . . . so what . . . sure, a tunnel . . . nonchalant.

My dad came back soon with a letter in his hand. "Special delivery," he said. "It's for you, Nicky. I s'pose it's you, though it says, 'Copin.' " He seemed mildly surprised.

I took the letter. It was a long white envelope, important looking, and I don't like the look of this sort of letter. I've had two from P.S. 2 in my lifetime, and the news in neither of them was good. For a time people forgot Minny down below and "Get me out of here," and "Help! Help!" They were curious about my letter.

Well, it is unusual for a boy of the Alley in Grade Six to get a special delivery letter, especially on a Sunday night. And especially when they saw where the letter came from . . . Gracie Mansion! For me, all right. Mr. Copin Carroll. It said it on the envelope. The only person outside the Alley who knows my name is "Copin" is the mayor. So, this letter was from the mayor, at last.

"Just a letter from the mayor," I said. "So what!"

I wasn't going to open the letter with all this many people crowding around. Pretending to be angry about nothing special, I stomped into my house followed by Tornid. I took the letter to the dining-room table . . . it was clean, no crumbs . . . and opened it with a real letter opener—I knew where it was.

The letter:

Dear Mr. Carroll:

Your plans suggesting the preservation and the future of the Myrtle Avenue El, naming it and the area all around it a landmark, are creative, imaginative, and intelligent. The 'Myrtle Avenue Feast Line' with a special restaurant in each station is unique. I know of no other such feast line in any city in the world. Let us hope New York can be first in this.

Of special interest, too, is your speculation concerning a lost tunnel in the Borough of Brooklyn. Please keep us posted. And we will let you know what the experts' decisions are regarding the El plan. Let us hope it is not too late. One thing we can be sure of . . . it is *not* too late for the Feast Line. With best wishes to your colleague, Tornid Fabian,

Sincerely yours,

Kenneth M. Woolsey

Hon. Kenneth M. Woolsey

"Doesn't write his name very well, does he?" said Tornid. "Can't read that name in ink."

"Nope," I said. "Grownups don't write very well. First they learn to write well. Then they get over it. Anyway, you can tell from the envelope, it's not a fake."

Then everybody had to come in and look at the letter. No one had had a letter from the mayor except John

Ives. But he gets letters from everybody, the U.S. Senate, the House of Representatives, the governor, besides the mayor, because he writes everybody all the time about how to vote or how they have voted, and complains or praises, if praise is earned.

"Why'd they send it special delivery?" asked Star.

"Says on the radio," my mom said, "that there might be a postal strike any day . . . maybe tomorrow . . . and he wanted it to get here."

I was in a daze. I had almost given up hope of ever hearing from the mayor.

What a day! Tunnel found! El plan liked, feast line liked . . .

"Neat work, Nicholas," my mom said. (She doesn't go for the Copin-Tornid aliases.) "Aren't you hungry? Have a snack."

I said OK. I was hungry—three times down in one day! I mean it. I was hungry and tired, and the big expedition—Descent No. 5—to come any minute now . . . I was resolved. The minute I'd had something to eat, then I'd broadcast my invitation. "Come one and all." Maybe that was the way to start it all off, the announcement. Most people had gone back out and regathered at the drain, resuming their interrupted pondering over the words below and should they call the police . . . that's what they were thinking now, because that voice yelling help, help, really began to sound like more than just me or the *grils* or Tornid.

The only ones left in the kitchen were the moms and dads and Tornid and me. I ate some coffee cake and had some non-coffee coffee . . . Tornid, coffee cake and milk.

Tornid's mom said, "I wish somebody"—she gave me and Tornid piercing looks—"would tell me what's going on around here. Where's the tape recorder? And what's this about a tunnel? What's the mayor talking about?"

"Well," I said to myself, "now's the time all right. Now's the time to reveal the secret of the under alley . . . the Tunnel of Hugsy Goode." Hard though it was to suddenly share Tornid's and my top secret findings, proving that Hugsy's ESP was perfect, I began. "One day, Tornid and me, we . . ."

But . . . just then, fate intervened again. The phone rang.

Chapter 28

The Phantom of
the Under Alley

My dad answered the phone. We all listened to see who it was. When we answer the phone in this house, we usually say, "Why, hello, so and so"—whoever it is, so the other people can listen or not but at least know who it is on the other end. "Probably Bombel," my mom said. (He's a professor in my dad's department.) "Probably more shop talk," she said, pouring herself a cup of coffee. "That's all you hear around here. Grandby, Grandby, Grandby."

We heard my dad's part of the conversation. It was not Bombel, so we listened. My dad's end went like this:

"Why, hello, Gladys. You did say Gladys? Yes, of course . . . haven't heard your voice in such a long time . . . yes, should have recognized it . . . yes. And how are you? And all the kids? Not kids any longer. Really! How does he like it? . . . How they grow up! Hugsy is a freshman at . . . where did you say? Oh yes . . . fine school, very fine school. . . . Oh yes, I have heard of it. Who hasn't? What? Hugsy? No-o . . . we haven't laid eyes on Hugsy since you all moved away from the Alley . . . must be eight . . . nine, really! . . . years ago. How time goes. Hugsy? No . . . he hasn't been here. I'll ask the others." (Dad turns to us at the round table, asks, "Have any of you seen Hugsy Goode?" The moms shook their heads, no. Tornid shook his head no. "I never ever saw him and wouldn't know him if I did," he said. My jaw hung open, and thoughts of the phantom raced through my head.) "No," says my dad. "Well," he says, "you know how young people are . . . say they're going to do one thing . . . do another . . . not intentional . . . forgetful. Oh . . . said he wanted to visit his old haunts in the Alley? Well, if he comes, we'll get in touch. . . . Our best to . . . yes, we'll get him to call you . . . if he comes. Yes . . . want to speak to Latona? Oh, yes, you run . . . cats do get in fights. Come over, soon, yourself, all of you. . . . Bye. . . . Oh yes . . . better go quickly. Yes, we'll remind Hugsy of his date if he comes. Not likely to, this late, though. . . . That's right . . . never can tell . . ."

"Phew!" said my dad, mopping his brow. "What a talker . . ."

"Always has been," said my mom. "I take it it was Gladys Goode?"

"Yes," said my dad. "She thought Hugsy was over here . . . he'd said he thought he'd like to revisit his old haunts . . . the Alley . . ."

"Hugsy Goode?" said Tornid, puzzled. "Over here?"

"Oh, you wouldn't remember him," my mom said. "He used to live in your house before you moved in."

"Oh, I know him. I've never seen him, that's all," said Tornid. "He planted our peach tree . . . planted the squash vines over the hidey hole . . ."

I kicked Tornid under the table to make him shut up. My heart had begun to beat very hard. My mind was in a daze. Could Hugsy Goode's mother have some ESP, too? Maybe it runs in families. I gave Tornid a signal— three small taps on the ankle bone. It means, stand by . . . and I said . . .

"Mom," I said. "On the way home from the library, I

—Tornid and me—dropped my fountain pen. (Cross fingers, excuse the lie.) Could we just take a quick look? Be right back. I thought I heard something drop outside Mrs. Stuart's house . . ."

"Yes," said my mom. "But hurry right back. I'll leave the front door unlocked so you don't have to ring and wake up the baby. Now, hurry, I mean it . . ." My mom was sort of basking in the pride of having a son who, in spite of being awful, had had a letter of praise from a mayor, especially an intelligent mayor. But you could see she thought there might be some sort of catch to the whole thing and was playing it safe when she added, as we went out the front door, in her usual snap-the-whip tone, "Hurry, Nicholas. I mean it! Now, git!"

We got! We quickly retrieved our shillelaghs and gear from the ivy in Jane Ives's front yard and raced to the Alley gate with it all, pushing it under. Then we climbed over the Alley gate. We have done it many times and know not to tear our skin on the rusty barbed wire. Then we raced to the hidey hole, and we put our gear where we always put it. Then we raced back and up and over the Alley gate and through our front door. The moms and dads were still chatting and had already forgotten all about Hugsy Goode and did not think it odd at all he was supposed to have come over here to the Alley for a visit—an old-folks-at-home sort of visit—and had never shown up.

It was almost ten o'clock. "Mom," I said.

No answer. "Mom," I said again, and stood right beside her, and she looked at me, and we smiled our cracked-grin smiles we reserve for each other. And I said, "Mom, could Tornid and me go out in the Alley for a little while? It's hot. See how hot I am? (I showed her my beady face, and Tornid wrung sweat off his.) There's no school tomorrow. We'll just sit in the tree house, or—be right somewhere, some cool place, in the Alley."

The two moms exchanged glances, and the dads continued the conversation about the troubles of the school . . . and the moms, having the ESP between them, agreed by way of their ESP that we could go out to cool off in the Alley. "But—only for one half of one hour!" said my mom in her normal "or it will be the worse for you" voice. The letter from the mayor? Forget it! She has!

"Come on," I said to Tornid, once we were outside. "We have to hurry. Hugsy Goode is missing . . ."

"I thought," said Tornid, "Hugsy Goode was just someone from olden Alley times."

"Never mind what you thought," I said. "He is a real live guy—or was, until recently—a boy about my age. Oh, no . . . that is what he was when he lived here and planted the peach tree. . . . Now, oh holy cat, he's grown, has a beard they say. Tornid, old boy, old boy. That guy that was sitting in the Throne of Hugsy Goode this evening—well, that guy may have been Hugsy Goode! By now, the skeleton-maker may have made a skeleton out of him. Poor Hugsy Goode! At least we have his voice on Blue-Eyes' tape recorder—his last words taped on mini tape. Now, Tornid, you and me have to recover the mini tape recorder, restore it to Blue-Eyes, and let the mother of Hugsy Goode hear Hugsy say, 'Get me out of here!'—his last words."

"I don't want to go down there," said Tornid. "It's not my tunnel. It's the Tunnel of Hugsy Goode. It's time to tell the moms. And dads. I been down there a million times today."

"Crud! We're just going as far as the chair and get the recorder. Rush right back. By now, the skeleton-maker is probably in one of the places of business we haven't had time to locate yet, has probably lugged Hugsy off with him to make him into a phantom, the phantom of the alley under the Alley. He will be a legend, Hugsy will—the legend of Hugsy Goode. A Brooklyn legend."

Tornid still didn't want to go. Who would? I didn't myself. But, follow things through to the end—that's my motto. And I just had to get the recorder and watch the astonishment on everybody's face when they heard the whole story of the Tunnel of Hugsy Goode. "Too bad he died," they'd say, "but you usually name tunnels and bridges after dead people, anyway, not live people."

After that, they'd call the police, I thought, or somebody, to ferret out the smoogmen, or the skeleton-maker, so the tunnel would be safe for processions and such. This thought made me happy, and a few words of encouragement convinced Tornid we had to get Minny. Calling his sister's recorder by this nickname made the whole expedition less dangerous, a family project, and we slid down the hole in the hidey hole. This descent is No. 5. The hole was much larger than it had ever been before, the dirt and loose rubble around it more crumbly than it had been even the last time down—Descent No. 4—a couple of hours ago.

We had traveled through Tornid's passageway and then around the bend into the top of the T and to the chair so many times, we hardly needed lights on. We had them turned on, anyway, to blind whatever or whoever needed to be blinded by them.

When we got within sight of the chair, no one was sitting in it, not Hugsy, not his phantom, not the raccoon, not even the mini tape recorder with its famous last words taped on it. Like it or not, we had to go farther. So on and up into the glooming we went. I had a terrible feeling of foreboding. Every few steps we paused and listened.

Then, from far ahead, perhaps at the under Circle, came a voice, hoarse and desperate. "Come one step nearer, whoever you are, and you'll get it . . ."

A voice! Could it be the voice of Hugsy Goode? Or—his phantom? Or Minny?

Chapter 29

The Voice of Hugsy Goode

"Listen! Whoever you are," came the voice from out of the glooming.

I clapped my hand over Tornid's mouth to keep him quiet while we listened and studied whose voice this was.

"Who's up there?" asked the voice. "I'll tell you who I am . . . I am Hugh Z. Goode. I used to live in the Alley. I fell through some . . . hole and landed in darkness. I bumped my head, I lost my bearings . . . can't see anyway, and I don't know where I am. I must have freaked out. Get me out of here, please. I have a date in Paterson . . ."

"Come slowly, with your hands up!" I said. "Take ten steps." To Tornid, I whispered, "Keep mum. It may be an impersonator—the skeleton-maker, some creepy smoogman. Raise your shillelagh. Be on guard for anything."

"I hope I can still count," said the guy. "I may have a concussion. I can't hold my head up . . . it keeps hitting something. I'd sure like to know what sort of thing I'm in. One, two . . ." and on up to ten he counted.

Whoever this guy or smoogman is, he is awfully tall, I thought. . . . Tornid and me took ten steps, too. So then all of us were twenty steps nearer each other. Now we could barely distinguish his form way up at the Circle, preserved in the under alley though not on top. His hands were up, and as far as we could see, he didn't have any weapon. I whispered to Tornid, "We have to be sure this is the real Hugsy Goode, not his phantom or a guy that could strike us dead at a glance and then make a skeleton out of us."

The guy couldn't see us behind our lights unless he had the beam type of eye that can penetrate everything. "Hey," he said, "whoever you guys are, get me out of here, will you? I'm confused. Is this some sort of tunnel? Or what?"

"Freak out, man," I said. "You can't fool us. Hugsy Goode is a boy in Iowa . . ."

"Iowa! Crud! It's Michigan, man, Michigan . . ."

I whispered to Tornid, "It might really *be* Hugsy Goode, the real Hugsy Goode. After all, he thought up the tunnel. And we found it for him and named it after him. And now, after all these years, maybe this is him. . . . Tunnel's been on his mind all these years, maybe. And his mother did call in just now. But I remember him as just a boy—about my size that I am now."

Out loud, I said, "Come ten steps nearer. Keep your hands up."

We did the same. This brought all of us close to Passageway J.I. "Say, who are you fellows, anyway?" asked the guy.

"Don't tell him anything," I whispered to Tornid.

"Yikes!" said the guy. "What's that?"

Tornid and me jumped. We were more scared than the guy, but he may not know about smoogmen. Then I realized he was looking at the psychedelic head of the skeleton I'd drawn. "It's OK," I said. "It's art."

"That may be art," he said. "But now I've gone and twisted my ankle on some gol-darned tree trunk or something."

"Oh," I said. "That's just the leg of a skeleton."

"Say, who are you guys?" the fellow said. "Come on,

now. I'll make mincemeat out of you if you don't tell me who you are and how you get out of here."

"We're just two boys in a tunnel," I said. *"The* tunnel. I mean. The Tunnel of Hugsy Goode."

"Thanks a lot," said the guy. "But I'm in a hurry. I have a date in Paterson . . ."

"He must be real, the real Hugsy Goode," I whispered to Tornid. "Not his ghost. Because how would his ghost know about Paterson?" Out loud, I said, "My name is Copin Carroll."

"One of the Carrolls, eh?" said the guy. "I remember them. Don't remember one named 'Copin' though. Remember one named Nicky . . . he was just a baby, always had a rope."

"That's me," I said. "I changed my name to throw people off the track while Tornid and me were looking for and finding your tunnel."

"Who's Tornid?" asked the guy.

"My friend. His real name is Timmy Fabian. He lives in your old house," I said. "What'd ya do with the mini tape recorder? It belongs to Tornid's sister."

"Don't ask me," said the guy. "Some creepy thing came along, some furry thing, and grabbed it in his mouth and ran away with it."

"That's Racky," I said.

"Well, Racky must be a very bad character," said the guy.

"He's a raccoon," Tornid said. "Not a character. A sport raccoon."

By this time Tornid and me coming from down the Alley, and the guy, limping, coming from up it, were close to each other. I shone my light up at him. He had to stoop over he was so tall, too tall for a six-feet-high tunnel, and they must not have used to grow people that

tall except for Abraham Lincoln or they would have
made the tunnel higher while they were at it.

"You really Hugsy Goode?" I asked.

"Hugh Z. Goode," he said. "Same difference."

This being a saying of the Alley, we were now convinced, and it was very pleasant to have company in the
under alley. "How come you didn't recognize your own
tunnel?" I asked.

"I didn't have any matches or any kind of light. And
how come it's my own tunnel?" he asked.

So we told Hugsy how it was because of him, the words
he had said once—that there probably was a tunnel under
the Alley—that Tornid and me decided to find it. We had
lots of time, there was a strike on at school, and we didn't
have to go, which was convenient.

"No one but us, Tornid and me, and now you, know
about this tunnel so far . . . oh, and Racky. We don't

know yet whether there are any inhabitants down here—smoogmen, skeleton-makers, or what. But so far we haven't met up with any of them, though they might be watching us all right now, from one of the dens or offices . . ." I said.

"Cripes!" said Hugsy. "Fantastic!" he said, and his voice cracked, he was so amazed. "It's just like the Alley on top?" he asked.

"Yes," I said.

"Like looking in a pond and seeing a reflection of the Alley . . ." he said.

"Only we're right side up," said Tornid.

"I hope so," said Hugsy. "But let's get out of this creepy place."

Hugsy's ankle hurt him, so I gave him my shillelagh to lean on, and Tornid gave him his to feel the wall with if he wanted to feel the wall.

I said, "This small passage is the J.I. passageway—J.I., named for Jane Ives . . ."

"Oh, I remember her," said Hugsy. "And Connie . . . wonder where she is . . ."

"Out," I said. "And this J.I. passageway leads under Story Street and all the way to Memorial Hall and goes on to the library."

Suddenly Hugsy's ankle felt better. Hearing the old landmarks mentioned, he felt as though he were near to civilization. He didn't have a see-in-the-dark watch with days on it and also a compass. "What time is it?" he said.

"After ten," I said. "We have to get back."

"What day is it?" asked Hugsy.

"Sunday," I said.

"Still Sunday, at least," he said. "Cripes, even so, I've been down here a couple of hours."

"I know it," I said. "We saw you . . . it was around nine o'clock . . . on the chair . . ."

"Saw me? And left me down here?" he screamed.

"We thought you were a phantom or a skeleton-maker . . ." I said. "I'm sorry."

"OK," said Hugsy. "But I sure never expected to slide down a hole in my own old-time hidey hole when all I was doing was remembering old times. Cripes! Now I know how Alice felt in the rabbit hole." He pinched himself. "You sure this is all real?" he asked. "I did bang my head . . . this tunnel's too low. . . . You sure this isn't a dream?"

"Oh, no," said Tornid. "It's real because we're here."

Then Hugsy said how, in a daze, after falling into this place and knocking his head on the top of it, he had stumbled along and stumbled upon this chair, and it gave him courage. A chair must be somewhere, he thought, where people are. So he wriggled his way into it . . . and fellows . . . it was dark! Then he felt he was sitting on something, and he felt it all over and he said, "I once had a mini tape recorder, and I pushed the button, and darn if this thing didn't start saying things, so I added my two cents, hoping I'd be heard by somebody who'd come and get me out of here." He felt his head. "I might have a concussion," he said. But he said he felt OK and that he would like to follow through the J.I. passageway and see where the entire thing wound up, since, according to us, he had been the thinker-upper of the tunnel in the first place.

"We've named the tunnel—the Tunnel of Hugsy Goode," said Tornid.

"Well . . . gee . . . thanks," said Hugsy the Great.

So we all headed down the J.I. passageway. We knew

our parents, though worried and not even hearing Minny giving out reassuring messages, would soon feel very happy when they learned we had found and rescued Hugsy Goode, who'd missed his date in Paterson, N.J. Now, the only thing wrong was that I didn't have the mini tape recorder to hand over to Contamination Blue-Eyes. "Let's call it quits," I'd say, "us calling you and Black-Eyes 'Contamination.'" "OK with me," she'd say. Now, I couldn't do that. She would still think I had stolen it and hidden it some strange somewhere. Anyway, a real alive missing person, six feet, three inches high is more important than a mini tape recorder, and they'd all have to be satisfied with that . . . just plain Hugsy Goode.

On the way up Passageway J.I. to the door marked Memorial Hall, Hugsy said, "I never did like dark tunnels." And he said, "I have always had a sort of claustrophobia." And he said, "Ow," often because he would forget to stoop. And he said, "You sure you know where we're going?"

Finally we reached the door. Triumphantly I shone my light on the sign on the heavy door labeled Memorial Hall. Tornid and me hadn't locked the door when we were here before and I didn't need my key, and this time it swung open more easily. We went at a fast clip now to get to the door marked Library. I tried to open that door. Yechh! It was locked. Someone had come along and locked it—we hoped it was Tweedy. But . . . it might have been someone or other on this side, not the library side, that had locked it. I felt uneasy. I searched my gunny sack for the big key. Gone! It might have fallen out in the Iveses' ivy.

No matter what, we had to go back the way we had come, through Passageway J.I. and to the Throne of

King Hugsy the Goode. No need to be scared, I said to myself, with the real Hugsy along with us . . . just so long as no one has blocked up our only escape route that we knew about . . . the hole into the hidey hole. Because now we didn't even have the mini tape to send up SOS calls. Well . . . there were still our own voices and the jump-rope chants—that's something. But I felt scared. I hoped Hugsy didn't. I flashed my light on the wall in the J.I. passageway where I had written *"Courage, mon ami."* Hugsy said, "Very good French . . . not one mistake."

But I was scared. I thought I heard sounds. So, before going out into the main part of the under alley, while still in the J.I. passageway but at its beginning, I said, "Lie low, fellows. I think I hear something, something from up near . . . I think . . . the Circle." A sickening feeling of foreboding swept over me. Here I was about to rescue a real live Hugsy Goode. Instead, now here the three of us were, about to face an unknown new peril.

Chapter 30

Music in the Tunnel

I spread my arms across the entrance of the narrow J.I. passageway so my friends would not panic and race into some trap, some unknown danger. I covered my light with my sweat shirt and turned it backwards, not into the main tunnel. Suddenly we heard, we all heard, the sound of music.

"Ha-ha," said Hugsy, and gave a nervous chuckle. "Where's that music coming from?"

"Must be the mini tape," I said, and gave a nervous chuckle myself.

"Racky must have come back to the throne and somehow set Minny going again. He is a smart and sport raccoon," said Tornid.

"Doesn't sound like anything that was on the tape before," I said. "Unless you sang into it, did you?" I asked Hugsy. I didn't know whether to call him Hugh or Hugsy or Mr. Goode or what, so I didn't call him by name.

"Sing! Ha-ha," was all he said.

"Sounds like a choir, or something . . . a ghost choir, maybe," I said.

"Hey," said Hugsy Goode. "This whole trip is giving me the creeps, and I have a date in Paterson. . . . Let's get out of here. Let's run for it."

We couldn't run, though. Hugsy's ankle still hurt too much. Anyway, the music sounded louder. The acoustics were almost too good down here . . . we could be drenched in music. I was scared. I turned off my flashlight and stuck my head out in the main under alley. I didn't see anything. I turned my light on again and flashed it at the psychedelic head. There was a word written in just plain white chalk under the head, and the word was HA-HA. Tornid and me had not written that word.

Hugsy's foot hurt, his head ached, his neck ached from stooping. He sat down on the floor a minute to rest. He didn't think there was anything odd about seeing HA-HA on a wall. Said people are always writing HA-HA and other words on walls. He just hadn't taken it in that, so far, only me and Tornid and, now, him knew about this tunnel. I began to get mad. Some nervy guy had written HA-HA in lots of places on my wall. When I flashed my light to right and left, I saw that everywhere Tornid and me had drawn an important arrow or direction . . . so many feet to here, or to there—someone had written HA-HA.

"The skeleton-maker?" asked Tornid.

"Doesn't seem like something a maker of skeletons would do—write lots of ha-ha's on Hugsy Goode's wall, and not even in good chalk, not psychedelic chalk, just plain chalk. Besides, where's the mini tape recorder, anyway? Where'd Racky go with it?" I said.

Hugsy said, "If Racky is as much of a sport raccoon as you've made out—likes the underworld better than the world on top—maybe he could have written HA-HA, too, and also recorded a choir of those guys—whatcha call 'em—smoogmen, a choir of the under alley."

This sounded like the old Hugsy Goode, the boy I remembered from long ago who'd had the ESP about the tunnel, and not some college guy with a sore ankle and a bumped head, late for a date in Paterson, N.J. I listened carefully to what he said for some sign of the old ESP.

Then my flashlight conked out—battery gone. All we had now was Tornid's feeble one. If we wanted to get back, we should go now before his conked out, too.

I said, out of respect for possible ESP of Hugsy Goode, "If that music we hear from far away is really a choir of smoogmen, it shows—it *is* still Sunday—that they are in their music den, making music and not dangerous now. Am I right?" I asked Hugsy.

"Sounds right," said Hugsy. And he said, "You and your friend are good explorers, good charterers of expeditions."

"Like Mr. Jenks and Mr. Lee," said Tornid. He laughed his first laugh. He felt safe. In the dark he could almost think Hugsy was his father—he was that tall. And home was just around two corners—no, three, and then his mom and his dad.

"Do you think you can walk, hobble, now?" I asked Hugsy. "Or I could get my dad to help. We're going to tell them about the tunnel the minute we get up . . . will they ever be surprised!"

"Great!" said Hugsy. He stood up. "I do want to be on my way . . . date in . . ."

He didn't finish. From up the under alley, the Circle end again, there came words now, not music now, not smoogmen choir. These were real live words spoken by live somebodies . . . perhaps thieves who'd stolen rare books from the Grandby Library. That new thought struck me now. Someone had locked the library door to the tunnel. Who? Book thieves?

"Get behind me," I said to Tornid and Hugsy again. I was determined, now that we had found Hugsy alive, to get him back alive. "My shillelagh," I said. Hugsy handed me mine. "Lie low, you guys," I said. "Don't say anything, not even anything funny."

Then I whispered to Hugsy Goode, "Me and Tornid never met up with anybody down here before you . . ."

Suddenly a whole lot of lights came twinkling on, way up at the Circle end of the tunnel. We couldn't see who was behind the lights. "Turn your light off," I told Tornid. He did. All three of us . . . never mind the generation gap . . . crouched in the dark entranceway marked J.I., hoping the invaders—or tunnel occupants—would not come our way.

Now. Now, I thought, now we'll see who occupies this tunnel. Having a college boy with us, beard and all, even one with a twisted ankle and bumped head, I felt brave. *"Courage, mon ami,"* I whispered.

Chapter 31

The Invaders of the Tunnel

Tornid and me and Hugsy Goode—we were still crouching down close to the J.I. wall—we lay low and listened.

"Sh-sh-sh," said a voice. "They went in there . . ."

"You must have been mistaken, Beatrice. You always think you hear sounds . . . even in the attic, let alone a neat tunnel like this."

A familiar voice, but it might be a put on—smoogmen imitating voices from the world above to deceive us. The next comment persuaded me it was not a put on.

This voice said, "No, Izzie. I'm zure I heard zoundz. Not the mini tape . . . we have that, and it iz played out, nothing after it zaid, 'Get me out of here.' "

That was the voice of black-eyed *gril*. Fright had brought on a relapse into the "z" habit.

A quavering voice said, "I wish I hadn't come."

"Play it's Halloween, only without a moon. And I am a ghost," said a little whispering voice.

"Holly!" I whispered to Tornid.

The next voice said, "Are we all here?"

That was the voice of Bayberry Fabian. The little lights and the voices were coming nearer. Tornid's mom was in front, the *grils* on each side of her, LLIB and Danny on each side of Tornid's dad. Then my dad holding Holly's hand, and my mom with all the rest of us except Branch, the baby. Who was minding him? I wondered. Maybe

Lucy's mom, she has claustrophobia. My mom had her cow horn and suddenly blew a blast on it. It was enough to shatter your eardrums. She wanted to make the little ones feel at home, but instead it scared some and Holly cried. At least my mom and Tornid's mom didn't whistle their piercing whistles. When eardrums began to open up and people to recover, Danny or Star or Steve would write something on Tornid's and my—no—Hugsy Goode's tunnel wall. LLIB wrote LLIB. So that was where the HA-HA's had come from, not from some smoogman or somebody.

Can you beat that? Writing words like that on our tunnel wall with the person we named it for crouching beside us right now and with a sprained ankle besides, also a bruised head. Yechh! Tornid and me had to get the upper hand again of the affair of the tunnel. They'd gone and spoiled all the fun of Tornid's and my surprise, these . . . these . . . invaders had!

Now, the troupe had gotten down to the throne, pausing only long enough to write their HA-HA's. I got more and more boiling mad. All this was just the opposite of my plan. I had wanted to show them the tunnel, and now they had invaded it. I had planned to deliver Hugsy Goode to them alive and well, also the Minny. Now they had that, and they had all spoiled everything. I could even hear what they were saying in this glooming that used to belong only to Tornid and me—and now Hugsy, of course.

I heard Contamination Blue-Eyes say she must sit a minute, she was feeling faint, she wished she hadn't come. Even the mini had not been worth that much to her—she could have saved towel wrappers again and gotten another mini next year. She asked couldn't they all get out now, or someone get her a glass of water. And she slid into the Throne of Hugsy the Goode. In old books they would have said "swoon," but this is not an old book, this book is of now.

The sight of Contamination *gril* Blue-Eyes swooning in the Throne of Hugsy Goode made me madder than ever. So I bellowed with all my might, "Don't sit in that chair!"

The effect was electric. Blue-Eyes leaped up as though she had sat on a porcupine, swoon forgotten. Bayberry Fabian said, "Lights out!"

Then I said in a sepulchral voice, as though my words were being spoken by bones, "Who wrote the HA-HA's on my wall? Who wrote the HA-HA by my head? Where's the rest of me?"

"That's not Jimmy Mannikin," said LLIB. "He's a good guy. He doesn't scare people."

"Whoo-oo?" I said. I was happy because I was in charge of the tunnel again.

No one answered. Just a bunch of whispers coming from up there by the throne. Hugsy Goode realized he was caught in the middle of some sort of Alley feud. He whispered, "This is better than the game of Meece when I was a kid in the old days of the Circle in the Alley."

"Hey, you all down there!" Hugsy Goode himself spoke, suddenly, in a normal Hugsy Goode voice, not sepulchral, not bone tones.

No one answered him. We heard, "Get behind me and Latona." The dramatic voice of Tornid's mom. "Or behind the chair."

We flashed Tornid's pale light down there and saw them all crouching. The moms still had their garb on, so they shielded lots of people behind their skirts. Then Bayberry said, "Come out. Come out wherever you are!" Then she said, "Now! Everybody! Lights on! Get ready to charge!"

We stepped out into the main tunnel. We were not scared any longer. They all turned on their lights. Right on us. What a crowd, Jane Ives, too! You would think we were on television or something. Maybe that's what Hugsy thought. He said one day last spring at college he was on television—some guys wanted to know about the generation gap. And now he said, in case it were television, "Thank you, thank you all, for this unusual and spectacular welcome back to my old haunts in the Alley. I have enjoyed almost every minute of it." He stood up straight, forgetting the ceiling. "Ouch!" he said. Our tall dads kept forgetting to stoop, too, and the three of them kept rubbing their heads.

The voice of my mom now. "That sounds like Hugh Goode."

"Oh, yes," said my dad. "His mother . . . Gladys . . . did phone. Remember?"

"Oh, my gawd, I sway-er!" said Tornid's mom. This was an expression she picked up in Vermont last summer, and it was not, in their family, considered swearing . . . just a folk saying.

Now, what do you know about that? Hugsy Goode really thought I had planned this royal reception in the tunnel in honor of his homecoming to the Alley! "Nick—I mean Copin," he said, "you could write the mayor and have this place made into a landmark. I've never seen a tunnel alley under a real Alley before, and I've seen many campuses, and some have an alley—but none as good as this one. So, thank you, thank you all," he said to the throng at the throne.

The mayor himself could not have spoken with more polish, and here Hugsy was, a college boy with a bruised head. He deserved having the tunnel named after him and also the chair. It's nice to have been the one to think up a great thing like this tunnel, and fine to be able to make a good speech to say thank you when honored.

Then everybody swarmed toward us. "Nicholas! Explain," said my mom.

I didn't know where to begin, so said nothing. But Hugsy was warming up to the whole thing. He hobbled to his chair named after him, saw his name written over it in psychedelic chalk, sat in it since it had his name over it, didn't mind the HA-HA written over his name, said jesters through the ages have done that, said he was in dramatics at school and enjoyed playing the part of king of the under alley. He usually was given the part of an old man in a boat . . . at school.

"This is better than off-off Broadway plays," he said, and lounged on his throne with his long left leg over the arm, to rest it.

Holly came up to Hugsy Goode and said, "It is Halloween. We are all ghosts."

Lucy, who is always exact, said, "Ghosts—but not in ghost costumes."

Hugsy Goode stood up a moment, waved my shillelagh —I hope he doesn't forget to give it back to me in the end —and said, "I dub you all knights and ladies of the under alley," and sat back down again.

"Well, boys, where does this all go?" asked Bayberry Fabian, her voice cracking a little the way Tornid's does sometimes.

"We'll show you," I said.

So, now at last, my dream come true—me and Tornid to lead an expedition of upper-Alley people through maze and tunnel to where me and Tornid know it goes. Hugsy Goode said he would stay on his throne because of his sprained ankle, that he had made the journey once already. "It's better than Disneyland," he said, "where things come out at you. And there are enough of you to scatter smoogmen to right and to left, nose them out of their dens, chase them and create chaos among their numbers."

"He should come back and live here," I whispered to Tornid. "The Alley would never be tame again."

"Yeah," said Tornid.

Leaving Hugsy on his throne—he said he might as well forget Paterson—with LLIB to keep him company, because he was too tired to go and wanted to stay with a king anyway, me and Tornid led off, my mom generously lending me her big flashlight. My mom and Bayberry sang. It was too bad we didn't have candles—it would have been prettier. But the flashlights cast a warm glow anyway. It was a friendly under alley, now. The moms borrowed our psychedelic chalk and wrote the names of all the children on their foreheads so they would not get lost.

Contamination Blue-Eyes had made a good recovery from her swoon. She had a spare mini tape for her recorder in her coveralls, and she taped us all as we strolled up the under alley, a record of the first group sing-in of the tunnel. It may be in the Grandby Library someday. If not, it should be. The moms sang songs like "Listen to the mocking bird, tweet, tweet," "If a body meet a body coming through the rye," and other songs suitable for the occasion. Then Bayberry sang, to please me and Tornid, finders of the under alley, "It's a long day's night." Not my mom, though, not even on this historic occasion would she sing Beatle. Yechh!

By this time we had gotten back to Passageway J.I., opposite which is Speciman A—the bone. I held up my hand for silence. (I may get a job as a guide someday in some park somewhere—it's fun explaining things.) "This," I said, "is where the skeleton, or the piece of it, is. The *grils* drew back in horror. They had not noticed Bone first time up . . . just saw my picture of his head and had drawn HA-HA over it. They said they would never have written HA-HA over it or over anything if they had realized what an important tunnel this was.

Feeling brave with all the moms and dads around, and with the guy who thought up the tunnel in the first place sitting down there on his throne, I gave the bone a big tug and it came out of the silt and I held it up, and it was a long, long bone.

"Hm-m-m," said John Ives, who had arrived home from his conference just in time for the descent. John is a learned man, but he did not recognize the bone. "I am not an archaeologist," he said, "just a professor of English

. . . and experts will have to do the real ferreting out of what bone this bone is. Too bad Professor Starr isn't here . . . he'd know." So we placed the bone carefully back under its psychedelic head for future scrutiny by an expert.

And he said, John Ives said, that he would ask the people at the Museum of Natural History to take a look at it, put it in one or another of their cases, identify it with name and place of discovery. Mrs. Stuart, who was born in Brooklyn and grew up here, said she thought the bone should go to the Brooklyn Museum or Historical Society. It was found in Brooklyn and belonged here, though preferably not so near the under alley of *her* house. It was spooky having it right here, and she was glad she had not known about it all the years she lived here until this minute and her children grown now and off at college—so apt to have nightmares about it.

What a stream of learned men would be coming down to Tornid's and my tunnel to look at the bone! Right here's where I could be a boy tunnel guide, not at some faraway park, I and my pal, Tornid, guides of the Tunnel of Hugsy Goode.

Next we went on up to the Circle. Even though the Alley people had seen it, they wanted to see it again and reminisce about the one that used to be on top. Then we came back and turned into the narrow J.I. passageway.

"Creepy . . ." said Bayberry Fabian, and Blue-Eyes stuck right close to her to protect her.

"Now, we are under Jane Ives's house," I said. I gave Jane a grin. I couldn't help but feel proud. All those maps and mazes and plans, tunnel plans, drawn there, in her house, come true.

She said, "Copin. It's fantastic! Exactly as you and Tornid drew it. Exactly! Once I thought I heard you down here. I heard weird sounds. Were you? Was it you?"

I just gave her a wink . . . she couldn't see it, though
—it was too dark—so I said, "It was us."

Then on we went through Passageway J.I. amidst con-
stant exclamations . . . "To think you had the courage
to come through here, all by yourselves," and other grati-
fying words of praise, to which Tornid and me, though
the terror of our first trips down was well remembered,
just said, "Shucks, it was nothing."

When we reached the door marked MEMORIAL HALL,
"Well, I'll be durned," said Tornid's mom.

"It doesn't mean a hall in memory of the guys the
skeleton-maker made into skeletons," Tornid explained
to reassure his mom. "It just means Memorial Hall where
we go to the students' plays and dance concerts. You been
there often."

"I thought we were going to end up in the river," said
Jane Ives. "Some of your plans showed that that might
happen."

"It doesn't, though," I said. "Tornid and me've been
through that door and the next door, too. The next door
is a door into the library. We tried to get Hugsy out that
way. But somebody had locked it. And I dropped the key
somewhere, so now we can't get in."

"Mercy!" said Bayberry.

So we proceeded back through Passageway J.I. and,
singing, re-entered the main tunnel. Hugsy Goode and
LLIB were glad to see us, and we all went back to T.N.F.
and TRATS, and climbed out through the hole, big ones
boosting little ones who didn't want to come out. They
wanted to sleep down there, and Holly cried.

So there we all were then, in the Fabians' backyard,
and Hugsy couldn't believe the peach tree was the one he
had planted from a peach pit. But it was. The light from
Billy Maloon's back stoop, a powerful beam, lighted up

Tornid's garden, and we could see all of us and take count. No one was left behind, so the moms and the dads said they should block up the hole right now so little ones could not fall through it the way Hugsy Goode, a six-foot-three man in college, already had. But Tornid and me said, "We can't. Racky is still down there."

"Oh, no, he isn't," said Black-Eyes. "There he is! He's up in his mussy old nest."

Sure enough. There he was, all right. By the light from Billy Maloon's house, we could see his ringed tail. "Well, we'll fix that hole right now then," said my mom. She went home and came back with the huge piece of slate they'd chucked out of the Engineering School, and she placed it tight against the hole in the hidey hole, Tornid's and my private, until now, entrance into the tunnel. Now, no one could get in, or out—at least for the present. I felt sort of sad.

Tornid's mom said everybody should come into her house for coffee and cold drinks, and she had made a cake that morning. So everybody did. It was as good, better, than the long night of the raging river on Larrabee Street. Better, because then the tunnel was just an idea of Hugsy Goode with just a few chips chipped out of the wall. And now we had found it and named it.

I decided to speak to the *grils* since in the glooming below they had decided to speak to me. "How come," I said, "you knew about Tornid's and my tunnel? How come you waited until Tornid and me were out of sight and then you went down there and spoiled the surprise we had for everybody? No wonder Tornid and me have to call you 'Contamination.' "

"Yeah," said Tornid. "That was sneaky. Not nice . . ."

"Not sneaky at all," said Black-Eyes. "So there!"

Blue-Eyes, now that she had her mini tape recorder

back and it was not broken, spoke more gently. She said, "Not sneaky, really, Copin. Not sneaky at all. While you and Tornid were wherever you were just now . . ."

"They were finding me," said Hugsy. "And I might as well skip Paterson . . ."

"Yes. While you were finding Mr. Hugh Z. Goode . . . only we didn't know anything about all that at the time . . . Beatrice and I came out to cool off in the tree house and look at the stars. I wondered," said Izzy Blue-Eyes, "if I would ever see my mini tape recorder again . . ."

"Yes, and . . ." interrupted Black-Eyes, forgetting she hated me, "just then by the light from Billy Maloon's back stoop, we saw the raccoon coming out of the hidey hole, and we were so excited because we haven't seen him in such a long time, and we could see he had something dangling from his mouth, so . . ."

"So . . ." interrupted Blue-Eyes. ("It's my mini and I should be the one telling the story," she gently reproached her sister.) "We could not help but say, 'Oh, look! The raccoon! And he has my mini tape recorder . . . holding it by the strap in his mouth. . . . It will get broken . . ."

"And . . . yes," said Black-Eyes. "That startled him and he jumped back into the hidey hole. The mini was saying, 'Coming, Mother.' That was not very nice of you, Tornid . . ."

"I'll pay for part of a new tape," I said.

"So, we went to the hidey hole and we found the recorder. You could tell where it was by the 'Coming, Mothers,' and we picked it up, still saying these words. We parted the squash vines carefully, but the raccoon was not down there. Still we had just seen him jump in . . . where was he? We felt all around . . . I hope they don't bite . . . but he just wasn't there. Isabel guarded the hidey hole, and I got Mommy and Daddy. And they found the big hole. And then we all got coveralls and went down. But as we went down, the raccoon—he jumped on Daddy's shoulders and went out."

I said, "We, Tornid and me, don't know where he used to go down there. We have only seen him as far as the chair. Shows there is more to this tunnel than Tornid and me have found yet. But Racky may have found it all, gone wriggling through one after another secret crawling-through passage . . . maybe over to Mike's art store . . . I just know there's a tunnel there . . . that may be the one that goes over to Myrtle Avenue. Maybe Racky's found the offices, the business places for the smoogmen, if there are any . . . their bunks, their things. . . . I've lots of plans and mazes . . ." I said.

Chapter 32

The End

We never got to explore again. The tunnel has been closed up tight. No one can get down there any more. They were afraid little children would slide down into it the way Hugsy Goode did, and he is not little—six feet three and only eighteen! So now the tunnel has been cemented up tight, and there is no use your trying to locate it, or our trying to locate the secret dens, if there are any.

But they didn't close it up until the president of the college had made the grand tunnel tour with Tornid and me as guides. He was flabbergasted at the whole idea of being president of a college that had this unique item. He looked at Bone and said he thought it was a leg bone of a horse. He had worked as a veterinarian once to earn his way through college and knew leg bones of horses. He sent the leg bone to the Museum of Natural History, though, for them to ponder and date, if possible. It was just as hard to figure how a leg bone of a horse got down in the Tunnel of Hugsy Goode as it was to figure how, if it had been a leg of a man, *it* got down there.

The president said, on his grand tour, it was lucky the students had never heard of the tunnel. They'd probably draw more than HA-HA's on the walls and giant footsteps on the floor. Then he and the librarian, Mr. Amos Belcher, Mr. John Ives, Professor Starr, the learned Grandby College professor of archaeology, Tornid and me, the discoverers of the tunnel, went down into the library basement, and these men studied old records and newspapers.

Mr. John Ives read something from long ago in a paper named *The Brooklyn Eagle* that told about this entire area. "Jackson's Hole" was the name of it then. "Belonged to a farmer named Jackson," Mr. John Ives read out loud. "Says, 'Jackson lost a mare named Milly down here once in the swamp.' Maybe that was Milly's leg you found in the tunnel," he said to us.

Tornid said, "O-o-oh," because he felt badly about Jackson's mare even though it all happened about a hundred years ago. I didn't feel all that badly. It's a Fabian custom to feel badly about all animals, not a Carroll custom.

Then those four men, the president, Mr. Belcher, Mr. Starr, and Mr. Ives, they all said "Whoopee!" at once. What they'd found now in some dusty box . . . Mr. Belcher said it was disgraceful, the condition of the basement, and you could see he hoped the president would not mind, or sneeze—Mr. John Ives sneezed, for he has many allergies and he sneezes loudly even at the word "sneeze" . . . the reason they said "whoopee" was that they found the architect's original sketches and plans for the Alley and the houses, in fact, for the entire campus, including the tunnels.

"Hm-m-m," mused John Ives. "Filled in Jackson's Hole with lots of tin cans, and that's what we're built on . . . tin cans . . ."

They had used the tunnel for special ceremonies, but they'd had to give that up because the tunnel was not tall enough for the tall professors, especially in their mortarboard hats. Besides, there had been a cave-in . . . "I told you there would be!" exclaimed John Ives, as though he were alive way back then and arguing then against the whole wild plan, especially in view of the tin-can base. "Just an eccentric scheme of some eccentric architect," he fumed.

"That's people," I said to Tornid. "Never like anything good! We thought it was neat. Even the *grils* did."

Anyway, no matter what we thought, they decided to seal it up after the cave-in, and from then on used only the tunnel that went under Grand Street from the library to Memorial Hall, and that only for processions when it was raining hard out. Mr. John Ives said he'd marched in it for his commencement in 1932!

As time went on, people forgot about the tunnel. Only Hugsy Goode had the ESP to think it up all over again, and Tornid and me to draw the logical plans and, best of all, to find it!

What became of the raccoon, of Racky? The chief zoo men of the city said that since this unusual raccoon was found in Brooklyn and helped to explore a tunnel on land that may be proclaimed a landmark—the landmark Tunnel of Hugsy Goode—his home should be the Prospect Park Zoo in Brooklyn. There he is. Go and see him, if you like. His name, Racky Fabian—since he was first seen looking in the Fabians' window, that's fair—is on his fence. You may not get to see him, though, because he spends much time digging himself a tunnel. There was a picture in *Life* of him doing this. It shows he misses his life in the under alley where it was nighttime all the time.

The Throne of Hugsy Goode? How about that, you ask? Well, they took it up and out through the tunnels and over to the library, and they had it all cleaned up and they put it in the hall of the library, next to the grandfather clock. You can sit in it—it is sturdy. Our—Tornid's and my—hunch about why it was down there was as right as any that anyone else could think up . . . that it may have been used by ladies of long ago to sit in if they got tired during the candlelight processions, or even as the throne for the crowning of the Snow Queen . . . some ceremony . . .

The librarian wanted to put a little plaque on the chair saying, "The Throne of Hugsy Goode." But Hugsy did not like that. "What would my friends back in Michigan think?" he asked. "No one calls me 'Hugsy' now."

They asked if they might name it, "The Throne of Hugh Z. Goode." At first Hugsy said no, he thought they only named chairs after dead people. But then he began to like the idea, for he saw that he is a sort of legend of the under alley and of the Alley on top, too. Besides he had a grandfather named Hugh Z. (for Zachary) Goode, and his friends could think it was his old chair. So that's the way it stood. You can go and see it, if you like.

The El? The "save the Myrtle Avenue El plan" or at least, if it had to be torn down like all other els, to turn the stations into international restaurants . . . a feast line? This is still being studied by the Landmarks Society of New York City. John Ives, who travels a lot, thought the idea was great and did some investigating. "Bills are still pending," he said. "So . . . who knows?"

Billy Maloon was a little jealous . . . Connie said this to us . . . because Hugsy Goode had a tunnel and a chair in the library named after him and Billy didn't, not so far, anyway, and he was eighteen, too.

Anyway, I wish this bill would get pended before August 4, my birthday and the day of another important event in my life and in life in the Alley. Important? How come? You say, why is August 4 important besides being your birthday? Well, I'll tell you why. We Carrolls, all of us six children, all born and raised here in the Alley, except for that one year in Mexico where Branch was born, are *moving!* To Vermont! Knock me flat! But it's true.

The only people in the Alley who know this big news are Jane Ives and Tornid and his family, outside of my family. My mom said not to tell every Tom, Dick, and Harry, so I didn't . . . don't ask me why. Moms and dads just like to keep things quiet. Then when the time is ripe, our mom and dad are going to tell it to the whole Alley, invite everybody in the Alley and lots of people out of it, even people they don't like, to a great big smashing farewell party they are going to give themselves, with pizza, salads, barbecued lamb, and such.

Tornid and me thought it would have been great to have the party in Hugsy Goode's tunnel, but it got cemented up first, and Tornid and I sure aren't going to chip it open again and show the sights down there. No, sirree. Too late, too hot . . . and the tunnel's bygone history, now.

I won't write a chapter about the party, when it comes. I'm winding this book up right here. Some other person can write the next annals of the Alley, not me. I won't be living here . . . we're moving to Vermont.

Oh sure, I'll miss my pal, Tornid. But he can come and visit me. We are going to have a house with thirteen rooms. There are more trees to climb there, more walks to walk. No locked gates.

I'll miss Jane Ives. I went over to tell her the news. My mom said, yes, I could tell her. I sat at her kitchen table the way I've done at some time every day for years now. It's Sunday morning. I had some sausage, a cup of my kind of coffee. I fixed it carefully the way I like it and I sipped it slowly . . . a teaspoonful at a time, and I added a little more sugar. And I reached my hand up from under the refrigerator door and took out an egg when she opened the door . . . and . . .

"What's up, Copin?" asked Jane Ives. "What's up?" Jane always knows when something's the matter or there's been a new twist. It's her ESP.

So I told her. "We're moving," I said. And I told her where, when, and how.

"I know how to make friends," I said.

She said, "I know you do. Get to school early the first day. Then you get to see everyone as they come into the schoolyard, and you don't seem like a new boy, then."

"Oh, I'll be the first one there," I said. "I know you don't go up to a kid and say, 'My name is Copin. What's yours?' That's dopey. The thing is to kid around for a while. Then it comes up naturally. You say, 'Well, so long. Be seeing ya.' And he says, 'So long. See ya.' Before you know it, you have a friend . . . you always have a ball in your hand or your pocket, in case he may want to play catch. I already have a friend. I saw a guy the day we looked at our house. He lives next door. He was looking through his window. We didn't look at each other. But we saw each other anyway . . . don't know his name yet.

"I'm going to have a room to myself there . . . there are so many rooms! Everyone will have a room of his own. You can come and visit . . . all the Fabians . . . Tornid . . ."

Jane said, "You'll love it, Copin. But I tell you, I sure am going to miss you and all our talk and your coming in and sprawling out, and playing Beatle records, and drawing, and scaring the bee-jeebies out of John or Connie when they come down to breakfast, hiding behind the television or somewhere, suddenly coming out, shouting . . . something . . . have them jump and clasp their hands over their hearts or ears. Well, we'll miss you. And the combine, the great combine of Tornid and Copin, the tunnel finders. . . . These days were great. Gee whizzee whiz whiz!"

Well, it was getting sad. So we were both glad when Tornid came in, hair slicked down, eyes shining, him smiling his wonderful smile.

Tornid said . . . he had some tomato juice—without Worcestershire sauce in it . . . he'd heard a boy was moving into our house, his name was "Sling." "I'll tell him about the good old days in the Alley when you and me found the lost tunnel," he said, "like the way you used to tell me about the good old days in the Alley when there was a Circle." And he said, "Maybe that guy you saw in that window in Vermont was Pete Calahan, the guy you wrote the ten letters for."

"Cluck!" I said. "That guy's out in Kalamazoo. And I never got one, not one letter, let alone one hundred! Yechh!"

In view of the important move soon to take place, Tornid and me have already stopped calling the girls *grils*. That was part of the tunnel game. Now we call Beatrice, Beatrice and Isabel, Izzy. My sisters, the same, though that was a harder switchover to make. Jane Ives said she had never liked the game anyway and was glad it was over and that it was a tie. Neither side had won or lost . . . the *grilz* or the *boyz* . . . as Beatrice might once have said.

Tornid said, "Where's Connie?"

"Sleeping," said Jane Ives.

"Sleeping!" Tornid said. I could read his mind. Here he had already been to church and to Sunday school and home again and now here for tomato juice and talk, and soon it'd be lunchtime in his house. There, meanwhile, upstairs Connie was sleeping.

Then, Tornid and me, we heard her stirring around up there. We hid between the linen cupboard and the television. Then Tornid and me shouted at Connie as she came past. She screamed. Then she laughed. She pretended to swoon. She has a nice laugh. I mean it. "You can tell Connie," I said to Jane.

Then Tornid and me said, "See ya," and raced out, leaving it to Connie Ives's mom to break the news of our moving to her and so that Connie could eat her sausage and waffles at my place at the kitchen table.

Anyway, it was time for Tornid and me to go home to lunch, my mom having come out to the back stoop and blown her cow horn. What will they make of the cow horn in Vermont, I wonder? *¿Quién sabe?*

I had my lunch, peanut butter sandwiches. Then I came

upstairs. And I sat on my bed. And I got this book out. It is fourteen notebooks full, and this is the last page of the last one. I figured it out just right. I thought of having to say good-by to Jane Ives and her kitchen and her dining-room table where all the plans were drawn. I hated to think of saying good-by to the Fabians, too, to my pal Tornid especially. I just didn't want to think about it. And I don't want to string this book along until that day and tell about it. And remember . . . I keep remembering . . . how it is you make friends. So, what I'll do is I'll say good-by to this book. So . . . now . . . I'm ended.

Write me if you like the book. Copin Carroll, Grandby College, Brooklyn, New York. They'll forward it. You don't have to Mister or Master me. I'm only eleven. But don't ask for my picture. I only got three of the P.S. 2 class pictures. I gave one to my mom. One to Jane Ives. The school kept the other for a scrapbook.

So, good-by. I sort of hate to write

THE END